VERY DEAD

"Johanna, it's Simona!" I called out, suddenly finding the silence of the apartment creepy. Across the street the Dakota loomed at me. I couldn't help thinking of John Lennon's murder and the witches' coven of *Rosemary's Baby*.

"Johanna, are you there?" I crossed the foyer, strode into the long corridor that led to the bedrooms, and knocked at a closed door. I got no answer and knocked again. Opening the door, I saw an overturned chair near the opposite wall. Her tortoiseshell brush sat on the corner of the dressing table.

My knees sagged when I finally saw her. Johanna was lying on her stomach in her glistening white bathrobe. Her face, pillowed by the thick white carpet, turned toward the bed. An inch away, a smear of pink lipstick stained the carpet, was looking like a last kiss.

I ran to the library and dialed 911. The operator kept asking me if I was sure she was dead. Calmly I told her, "Yes, she is dead. Very dead. Garroted dead."

A SIMONA GRIFFO MYSTERY

THE TROUBLE
WITH MOONLIGHTING

TRELLA CRESPI

ZEBRA BOOKS
KENSINGTON PUBLISHING CORP.

ZEBRA BOOKS

are published by

Kensington Publishing Corp.
475 Park Avenue South
New York, NY 10016

First printing: July, 1991

Printed in the United States of America

CAST OF CHARACTERS

in order of appearance

Simona Griffo   Transplanted Italian, too emotional to stay out of trouble

Sara Varni   Italian director, famous for her Leftist films, her crazy sunglasses, and her very bad temper

Massimo Marini   Movie screen spokesman for Italian male sensuality, who has finally decided to settle down

Sam Weston   Head gaffer on the movie set, who can sort out electric cables but not his own life

Johanna Gayle   Hollywood's latest golden girl, who has an odd concept of love

Diego Varni   Sara's husband, who prefers the risks of producing Leftist films to the stifling security of his moneyed family

Toni Berto   Still photographer on the set, who chooses good friends and bad lovers

Abe   Sam Weston's assistant, who sticks his finger into something hot

Barbara Walters   TV personality, famous for her intimate questions

Stan Greenhouse   Homicide detective, who isn't sure about all of Simona's troubles

Raf Garcia   Greenhouse's partner, who feeds Simona's hunger and curiosity

Jonathan Farnsworth *People* magazine reporter, who dreams of being the new Hemingway

Tiffany Seven-year-old girl, who may be Johanna Gayle's biggest fan

Bella SoHo artist, who runs a colorful Bed and Breakfast

Mahmoud Employee of the Majestic, who turns into a prince

Linda Shaw Johanna Gayle look-alike, name set who gets Simona's blood boiling

Plus an international assortment of film crew members, doormen, receptionists and passersby, who can always be found on the streets of New York.

Chapter One

Things were getting off to a fine start on my moonlighting job. I was standing on skyscraper-high stiletto heels, wearing a summer evening dress one choking size too small and being sprayed by the windswept fountain mist at Lincoln Center on an unusually cold September midnight.

"*Cazzo!*" Sara Varni, the Italian director, screamed from her perch on a crane thirty feet above ground. My sentiments exactly. Johanna Gayle, latest golden girl of Hollywood, had just interrupted the take one more time.

"Is *cazzo* Italian for 'cut'?" asked an extra, an older woman dressed in gray chiffon with bare arms prickled by goose bumps.

"No, it's a dirty word," I said.

"It means peeenus," Massimo Marini said with his strong accent. He was standing next to me, smiling at the woman while she blushed. For twenty-five years he had represented Italian sophistication and sex appeal on movie screens around the world. Coming from his mouth, a dirty word seemed lined in silk.

"What now?" Sara yelled through the megaphone at Johanna. Johanna ignored her, accepting Massimo's tuxedo jacket on her shoulders with a graceful sideways lean.

We were trying to immortalize the master shot of scene 14 of *Where Goes the Future?* Carole, the ace reporter for *The City,* is standing with a crowd of journalists and onlookers next to the round fountain that dominates Lincoln Center Plaza while the Italian prime minister walks by to attend a gala performance of *Tosca* in his honor. Carole, that is, Johanna Gayle who was playing her, is supposed to "accidentally" fall into the fountain and emerge shimmering with water, her jersey dress clinging to her underwear-free body. Johanna, whose body had the combined stopping power of Superman and Batman according to *Playboy,* had found some excuse not to fall in with each take.

As the crane lowered Sara down, the crowd of extras shuffled their feet on the pavement, which had been wetted down to give off the necessary sheen for the camera. Massimo, looking incredibly debonair in his shirt sleeves, didn't seem in the least bothered by the interruption.

"In anger Italians scream 'peeenus,' Americans 'fack,' " he said, tucking his arm under the chiffon lady's arm. She looked pleased. "Active verb: 'fack.' " He tightened his grip. "Go, go, go, that is the American way, is it not? Everything active verb." Massimo lowered his eyelids over the large, pale brown eyes that mesmerized so many women and smiled. "In Italy everything slow. Even 'fack.' Verrry slow." His free arm floated gracefully in the air as if he were trying to show us the rhythm for proper lovemaking.

Sara stepped off the crane with a "Johanna bella!" that could have shattered the glass front of the Metropolitan Opera House. She wasn't using the megaphone either. A menacing smirk crossed Sara's angular face. As usual her eyes were hidden behind custom-made sunglasses. That night she was wearing her crouching tiger ones, one eye peering through the tiger's face, the other through a haunch. The tail followed the curve of her eyebrows. As Sara, in black tights and an oversized black T-shirt, came nearer, I thought I saw the tip of the tail move, the cat about to spring. That's how tired I was.

It was my first day on the job as substitute dialogue coach after having left Italy — my home country — and the movie world three years ago. Faced with old friends and acquaintances, I was being whirled by confusing emotions of nostalgia, second thoughts about having left, even some fear of no longer being up to the job. I had also been recruited as an extra, which explained the high heels and the evening dress. I was in no mood to hear Sara's operatic explosion even if we were facing the Metropolitan. I had worked with Sara Varni, one of Europe's most famous film directors, several times. Her temper was atrocious.

"Sara, it's freezing," I said in a conciliatory whisper, coming out from behind Massimo. "Maybe if we took a break, Johanna could get warmed up." Not only Johanna. All of us. And I could get out of my three-inch heels. Forget about unzipping my dress and breathing; I'd never get back in.

Sara ignored me and walked her lean, muscular frame right up to Johanna, her black lizard boots scuffing against the wet granite pavement. They were soled by at least two inches of rubber to make Sara even taller than her five feet eight inches. Her tiger eyes reached the top of Johanna's blonde head. With Sara so close, Johanna backed into Massimo for some macho Latin protection. He rubbed her arm and closed his eyes. Massimo was not one for aggressive action.

"You fall in the water, or I push," Sara said, pointing a long, nail-bitten finger in Johanna's face. "You decide."

"Listen, tiger lady, I don't care how big you are back in pizzaland." The gaffer, Sam Weston, moved up through the crowd. "Here in the U.S.A., we treat people nice." He wedged his lineman's frame between Johanna and Sara. Johanna stared at Sam openmouthed, obviously not expecting a lowly gaffer to come to her defense. A gaffer is head electrician on a film, one of the toughest jobs on the set. Although he implements the ideas of the director of photography — DP in movie jargon — and is very important to the success of the film, on a big production he's supposed to know his place. He does *not* give orders to the director.

"If Jo don't want to get wet, then she don't," Sam said, crossing two beefy arms across his barrel chest.

Johanna visibly bristled at being called "Jo." "I can manage on my own," she said, leaning against Massimo even more. The wind had picked up again and blew her long blonde hair over her face. She sounded reedy and nervous; her famous dusky voice had disappeared.

Sara tensed, her body turning into pure gristle. She moved away from Sam. "For five million dollars, you manage as I say," she shouted at the top of her lungs. Then she did a 180-degree pan with her wide tiger face to include the two hundred extras huddled together for warmth. "She gets F-I-V-E M-I-L-L-I-O-N dollars for six weeks. You get thirteen dollars and twenty cents for the hour. But *she* refuses to get wet." Two arms flew up in the air. "American democracy!" One arm came down hard, pushing Johanna against the

10

black marble rim of the fountain.

Johanna stood up quickly, her face suddenly splotched with red, and ran toward her Winnebago parked straight ahead on Columbus. Massimo started after her, but Sara grabbed his shoulder to stop him.

"Simona Griffo, you know the Americans," she announced, jerking a thumb in Johanna's direction. "You talk to her."

Smoother hadn't been part of the job description I'd been given when Sara asked me to fill in for the regular dialogue coach who'd become too sick to come to New York for the last two weeks of filming. I expected to be translator of last-minute line changes for Johanna; English teacher and prompter to Massimo who spoke little English, had a transitory memory, and hated cue cards; and general go-between when language became a problem. Now I looked at Sara's black tiger eyes and shrugged. The problem between her and Johanna wasn't exactly one of language, but like it or not, I'd accepted the job, giving up two weeks of vacation time from my regular job at HH&H, a New York advertising agency. Remembering the nice fat check that was going to keep me in caviar for all of one second, I let Johanna run while I dragged my high heels in her direction.

The only thing I could think to do was apologize for Sara. "When she's on a film, she's people-blind."

Johanna, wrapped in a glistening white bathrobe, brushed her hair in front of one of six mirrors. "The whole world knows Johanna Gayle. Even in Bora Bora." Now that she was looking at herself, she ap-

11

peared calm. Her skin had turned back to its usual alabaster white. "She has an image to keep up. Intelligent, positive." That morning over a get-acquainted brunch at the Russian Tea Room I noticed Johanna always referred to herself in the third person. She sounded like a PR person pushing a product. As I stepped into the trailer, she leaned forward to examine a strand of hair, biting her lower lip when she spotted split ends. She had the old-fashioned, slightly plump beauty of Kim Novak and Marilyn Monroe, with the same air of vulnerability, and yet she had become famous playing feminist roles that required brains and feistiness. I watched her now happily indulge herself in her own image, like a child discovering a mirror, and wondered how brains and vanity mixed. Standing awkwardly by the trailer door, my feet hurting, I wasn't enjoying myself or putting my supposed knowledge of Americans to good use. Though we had barely met, there was something about Johanna that put me off, an unpleasant intensity, almost a greediness, that was not quite hidden by her intelligence or her soft beauty. It was like smelling a delicate perfume and then discovering a pungent, peppery aftersmell that caught in my throat.

"Johanna Gayle doesn't need to throw herself in a fountain to attract a man," she said. In the script, Carole was trying to get the prime minister of Italy, played by Massimo Marini, to notice her so that she could finagle a private interview. She had gotten wind that while he was in New York to address the UN, he would be approached by a special American undercover group. She wanted to find out why.

"Carole is highly motivated," I tried, stepping in and sitting down on a stool. "She wants that scoop at any price." I rubbed my arms to get some blood flow-ing. "Sara's films always deal with human weaknesses: greed, lust, ambition . . ."

Johanna arched her back as if she'd been whipped. "I'm not going to use my body that way," she snapped, throwing the brush on the carpeted floor. "She'll just have to come up with another way to catch the prime minister's eye. One that uses brains." Johanna glared at me from below thick black eyebrows, her anger very clear now.

The script was full of sexually manipulative scenes, so why had she picked on this one all of a sudden? I was willing to bet she was simply sick of Sara's dictatorial ways.

"She's so ugly," Johanna said, "all she can think of is the tits and ass she doesn't have."

"That is why she is the director," a polite baritone voice said from the opening door. "And you are the actress." Diego Varni, Sara's husband and producer of the film, stepped up into the long narrow space of the trailer.

Johanna ignored him and smiled at her reflection, her lips parting into red slashes that brightened her perfect teeth. She fluffed out her hair with a rapid wave of one hand.

"A woman must be confident to be complete," he said as he stooped down to pick up the tortoiseshell hairbrush. "Neither afraid of her brains nor of her beauty." Diego came from an old, moneyed Milanese family and spoke English with a crisp accent perfected during teenage summers spent in the English countryside. "I believe you strike a comfortable balance in this film." He held out the brush, and she started brushing her hair again with short jerky strokes.

He stopped in front of the stool I was sitting on,

13

one hand jingling change in his pants pocket. His square shoulders, widened by the trench coat poised on his back, made him look shorter and stockier than he actually was. Facing me with his square jaw, sharp jutting nose, brown hair cut very short, almost military style, he played the power role well. I wondered if he used the wide-shouldered trench coat to enhance that image.

"*Grazie,* Simona," he said, dismissing me with a curt nod. His eyes were so deeply set it was hard to see what color they were, let alone their expression. I was glad to get out of there even though I was relinquishing warmth and a place to sit. After my divorce, I had somehow lost my negotiating abilities.

Outside, I heard Sara with her megaphone rehearse the extras. Normally that's up to the assistant director, but Sara never thought he did a good enough job. She'd let him get the first words out, then she'd take over. The 12000-watt HMIs had been turned off. There were only a few smaller lamps on, running from a generator a few trucks ahead of Johanna's trailer. The drivers, all part of the powerful Teamsters Union, sat smoking and drinking beer.

"No, no, when she falls in the fountain," Sara's voice commanded, "I want a big 'aah,' then everyone away. Make a big hole so we see her. She will be like *Venere* . . . Venus born from the sea."

"She hates me." Johanna's husky voice wafted from the open window of her trailer like smoke. "She thinks I'm too stupid for her artsy fartsy film." She laughed. Diego's change jingled loudly.

"You are the one making difficulties," he said. "She is the one giving you five million dollars."

Great way of putting it, I thought, walking away. Diego's voice had all the warmth and lightness of cement.

Toni, the still photographer, met me underneath the portico of Avery Fisher Hall.

"Is she all right?" he asked.

I nodded. "Nice job you got me," I said half jokingly, as I took his leather jacket and flung it over my shoulders. Toni had been the one to remind Sara that I was now a resident alien in New York and could do the dialogue coach job even though I'd only done it a couple of times before. My specialty in Italy had been dubbing films. Most Italian filmmakers don't use direct sound in their movies; they rerecord everything. This allows them to use foreign actors who bring in much needed foreign money and sloppy scripts they can rewrite in the dubbing studio. I used to handle all that — organize it, find the actors, assist the director in the studio, oversee the sound editing and the final mix. Then my marriage fell apart, and I emigrated to New York where I'd gone to Barnard College fifteen years before.

I had dubbed three films for Sara in Rome, and we got along. I liked her films, liked her almost maniacal drive to make the very best; she liked me because I followed orders well, never letting her screams get to me. Sara said she was very happy I was available to take over as the dialogue coach in New York. I knew she was also thrilled to save the airfare.

"Sara's getting bad," Toni said, scratching his curly red hair. Toni was Sicilian (he claimed his red hair came from the Norman invaders back in the Middle Ages), short, covered with freckles, unlucky in love, kind, sensitive, a fantastic photographer who tried for cameraman and couldn't take the pressure, who loved film so much he happily scampered after movie stars all over the world, squeezing his chubby body into the

15

most absurd positions to get the best shots. We'd been very good friends for ten years.

"Sara hates wasting money," I said. "Do you have any idea why Johanna's holding up the shoot?"

"No," Toni said, looking very unhappy.

"Have she and Sara been fighting all along?"

"In Rome everything went as smooth as oil," Toni said. "It's America, I think. She's unhappy here." He wrapped an arm around me. "You convinced her to do the scene." He took it for granted I'd been successful.

For some misguided reason, Toni believed I had special knowledge of the world and that I could do whatever I set out to do. The good part was he never seemed disappointed when it didn't turn out that way.

"I barely opened my mouth," I said. "Diego's with her right now."

Massimo appeared from behind a column without warning. Toni dropped a flashbulb and I jumped.

"Mandrake," Massimo said with a chuckle, referring to the magician who had been one of Italy's favorite American comic strip characters back in the fifties.

"I wish you'd stop sneaking up on people. In New York it might get you knifed or shot," I said. "We're on the defensive in this city."

Massimo raised his hands in surrender. "Can't we cut the line, 'I thought that although'? " The "th" came out sounding like a "d" with a spit added to it. He smiled sadly, a trick he used on and off camera to seduce. I had dubbed many films with Massimo. There had been no heat between us, just mutual professional respect and some lighthearted fondness.

"Those words are imposseeble," he said in English, tilting his head to one side like a big, begging dog. I noticed how his good looks had slackened since I'd seen him four years ago.

"Go, go, go," I said, repeating his own words. I flashed my own smile, famous for getting me nowhere. "To do the impossible is the American way!"

Sam, an L.A. Rams cap shading half his face, walked by with a light stand over his shoulder. He poked Toni in the arm. "Hey, amigo, know how you can tell a producer's lying?" he asked in a gruff voice. "He's movin' his lips," Toni answered. They both laughed and walked off together.

"To your markers," the assistant director yelled through the megaphone. I gave Toni back his coat and walked quickly with Massimo toward our spot, five feet camera right of the fountain. I could see Johanna coming out of the trailer wrapped in a white fur. Diego walked behind her. The camera crane was lifting Sara, the cameraman, and his assistant up toward the sky. The wind, now blowing harder, cleared small patches of stars that would almost instantly be covered again by speeding clouds. The moon was hidden behind a skyscraper. All the lights came back on with a high-pitched, sizzling sound. I blinked from the brightness and wished I had Sara's sunglasses.

"What was her objection?" Massimo asked with his eyes closed. Makeup was hurriedly powdering his face.

"She wanted to use her brain to attract you."

"Is that so?" Massimo said, his sleepy voice looping softly upward. In real life, nothing seemed to perturb him; on screen, he became vibrant, essential. He had two Oscar nominations, three Best Actor Awards from Cannes, twelve Taormina Davids, and one Berlin festival Bear to attest to his past success. As I watched him saunter ahead to meet Johanna, I

17

thought that in the past few years that screen vibrancy had become less visible. Massimo was getting older and lazier.

He placed an arm around Johanna's white mink shoulder. They looked great together, each taking something needed from the other: she, Massimo's wearied, wise European calm, he, Johanna's strange American mixture of innocence and spunk. A couple of weeks ago I had seen their picture on the front cover of *People* magazine. LOVE REACHES ACROSS AN OCEAN, the headline had read. Underneath, in smaller print: "Macho Man Massimo Marini finally finds happiness with our own Gorgeous Gayle." They had been dating since the film began.

"*Signorina* Gayle, I compliment you on your feminist stand," Macho Man said. "About our lines . . ." Massimo walked Johanna out of earshot.

After ten minutes we were called to position. The camera started rolling, and Sara yelled out *"Azione!"* Massimo, with me and several others as part of his entourage, set out to cross Lincoln Plaza. The camera was first picking up the paneled glass front of the Metropolitan Opera House, behind which two giant bright Chagalls framed the chandelier that hung like a delicate upside-down sparkler between the curved double staircase. Then it was going to swoop down across the elegant crowd to the fountain in its full watery glory. Extras playing the part of Secret Service men tried to keep the press and the curious at bay. As the prime minister's party approached the fountain, I tripped over a feeder cable I didn't know was there. The actor behind me also tripped. I held my breath. Sara didn't call cut so I relaxed. Probably we could have all tripped, and she wouldn't have stopped the scene. She wasn't going to give Johanna a chance to change her mind.

"Your Excellency!" Johanna called out to Massimo in her role as Carole, *The City* reporter. "Can I have a word with you?" She had dropped her voice down between her legs and lifted one bare shoulder seductively. So much for the use of brains!

As called for in the script, Massimo waved his arm as if he were royalty and kept walking, with me and the rest of his entourage following. I heard a loud splash from the fountain, and I almost applauded. She had finally fallen in; two more hours to go and I'd be warm in my bed. The splash was Massimo's cue to walk back to the fountain. As he turned, I moved behind him so the camera wouldn't see me feeding him his first line.

"With all its riches, I did not know America also offered a Venus," I whispered.

Massimo said his line without a hitch, gallantly offering his arm to help Johanna out of the fountain. Johanna was going to answer with an enigmatic "That depends." She stood for a few seconds in all her dripping magnificence, looking incredibly happy about it all. Behind her, on the other side of the fountain, out of shot, I could see Toni bent over, snapping shots. Sam towered next to him, his gloved hands resting on his hips.

"This Venus isn't offering anything," Johanna said, dropping the smile and switching her voice to a no-nonsense mode. "And she can manage by herself just fine."

I winced at the line change, expecting Sara to screech "cut" any second. For some reason she didn't. Johanna proceeded to hitch her sopping jersey dress

19

up to her thighs. Ignoring Massimo's extended arm, she lifted one long leg to step over the marble rim of the fountain.

A loud, croaking gasp stopped her.

On the unlit side of the fountain behind Johanna, one of Sam's assistants stared at us with popping eyes, his mouth pulled back in an openmouthed black grimace. One hand was in the water. A second later he fell out of sight.

"Don't move," Sam yelled, running into the shot and pushing Johanna down into the water with a quick jab of his gloved hand. Johanna screamed.

"Don't get out of the water! It's hot! You'll fry!" Sam hopped in one spot, waving his arms in front of his chest. "No one touch her! For God's sake, no one touch her!" He sounded like a madman, the veins of his throat bulging out of his red neck. "That water's electrified!"

Johanna howled and jumped up.

There were gasps and screams from the crowd. Massimo reached toward her, and I hugged him by the waist. "Don't, please don't," I kept repeating, my face against his back.

Johanna extended her arms toward Sam. *"Nooo!"* he screamed.

I think I stopped breathing then, unable to tear my eyes away from Johanna. It was like watching an execution, waiting for the switch to be pulled.

"Cut the juice!" Sam yelled. "Cut it! What the fuck are you waiting for!" His massive body crouched down, gloved hands out in front of him. If Johanna tried to get out of the fountain, he was ready to push her back in, even at risk to himself. Crewmen were running, pushing extras aside, tripping over cables. One of them grabbed a walkie-talkie and rattled off some commands. Other men pulled at connectors. A few lights went out. Up on the crane, Sara shouted through the megaphone in the direction of the generator truck two hundred feet away.

"No light! Stop light! Stop!" Her third "Stop" fell in sync with the lights. Now only street lamps on Columbus and Broadway were on. A fraction of stunned immobility followed this sudden, calming darkness. Then Johanna doubled over, sobbing.

"Come on, you're safe now," Sam said, extending a thick arm to help her out. Johanna didn't move. "Trust me, if you fry, I fry. I'm the one touching ground." I looked down to see he was wearing rubber boots.

"Oh, God, make it go away," Johanna whimpered as Sam lifted her up in his arms and carried her toward her Winnebago. Toni ran to open the door for them. Massimo stayed behind, a baffled expression on his face as if he hadn't fully absorbed what happened.

"Go to her," I prodded.

He shook his head. "Later."

An ambulance siren pitched itself against the softer sounds of late-night Broadway traffic.

"Saam!" Sara bellowed from her perch thirty feet up. "How the *cazzo* do I get down from here?"

The ambulance crew examined the man who had been knocked unconscious by the shock. He was going to be all right, they reassured us, as they carefully maneuvered the wheeled stretcher between extras, crew, cables, and grip stands. The thick rubber soles of his boots had saved him.

Once the ambulance left, Sam took over. The Italian crew was too stunned to be much help. Even Sara, who normally thrived on crises, quietly waited thirty feet in the air while Sam cleared the area near the fountain, and the electricians scattered to check all the feeder cables that snaked from the generator truck to the lights.

Sam didn't make us wait long. "I found it!" he yelled from the shadows of the left side of the fountain.

I ran to where he was crouching, flashlight in hand. It wasn't far from where he had stood with Toni while we were shooting the scene.

Between his bent knees, under the flashlight's white circle, a two-inch-thick feeder cable touched the fountain's drain-off valve. Sam lifted the cable and turned it over.

"Shit," he muttered. The warm color of copper gleamed from a small gash in the rubber coating. Before I could see more, he put the flashlight down and quickly wound black tape around the opening, then used his teeth to break the tape off. He dropped the patched-up cable a foot away from the drain valve and stood up abruptly. I almost slipped as his shoulder pushed against me. The acrid smell of beer hit my nostrils.

"I got it figured out," he said to one of his men standing by. "A tear in the rubber exposed one leg of the cable, which would have been fine if four hundred feet hadn't pushed the damn thing against the drain valve."

"But the valve's ten feet away from the water!" I said.

"Yeah, the electricity shoulda have gone down to the sewer and blown the generators. I guess that sewer pipe wasn't grounded. Three hundred amps traveled

22

along metal piping to the water in the fountain. You can boil pasta real fast with that kind of heat." Sam wiped his face with his arm and pushed the visor of his cap over his eyes. "You can turn her on again. We're OK," he yelled out. He seemed to have no use for a walkie-talkie. Above him a huge drum-shaped lamp, a 200-lb. 12K HMI, flashed 12,000 watts of harsh light on Lincoln Center. It was like a small nuclear explosion. Everyone burst out in applause.

"Bravo, Sam," Sara's megaphone boomed, as the crane slowly bent its elbow to bring her down.

Johanna came through that early morning. After Sam proved the fountain was fine by putting both hands in the water and standing barefoot on the wet granite pavement, she redid the scene, master shot, medium, and close-up, using the new lines. She acted with riveting intensity as if the shock and fear she'd experienced had fueled all her senses. At the end, she won a round of applause from everyone, even Sara.

By the time we wrapped at four A.M., the media had got hold of Johanna Gayle's Close Escape from Death. Framed by the fountain's jumping jets of white foam, a towel-wrapped Johanna told the world how "deeelighted" she was to work with Italy's most famous director while a smiling, tiger-eyed Sara hugged her. Yes, she went on to say, she had felt a slight vibration as she hit the water but thought that was just some Italian goosing her. Everyone laughed while flashbulbs popped.

Massimo, on the other side of Johanna, displayed his sad smile, Diego jingled his change, and I wondered if he'd been the one to call in the press to turn the accident into a great publicity event. A tall, anchovy-thin reporter, a shock of straight brown hair dropping over his forehead and a pad and pencil in hand, slowly strode away from the main attraction in tattered, yellowed Keds. Sam, who was supervising the rolling up of the cables, saw him approach.

"I know nothin'!" Sam said loudly, turning his back to the man.

"How did that cable get nicked?" the reporter asked. He touched Sam's arm with his spiral pad. Without turning around, Sam flung out an arm, flicking the pad into the fountain. The reporter looked at his notes floating in the now turned-off fountain, then looked at the size of Sam's back. He gave a resigned smile, then threw his pencil in the water. I thought of Johnny Carson and the Late Show.

The actors and the press had left; the crane was slowly being pushed away; the fountain was still. Beyond the street lights on Broadway, I thought I saw the beginning of dawn.

"Forza, Toni," I called out, slipping out of my heels and unzipping my choking dress as far as was decent. *"Andiamo a casa."* It was time to go home.

Chapter Two

I woke up at one o'clock in the afternoon so groggy I barely made it down the ladder of my loft bed. I poured some fresh boric acid along the floor of the kitchen—a closet in one corner—and the tiny bathroom. The one-room apartment that I rent in Greenwich Village is really a time-share; I get the room in the daylight hours, the roaches take it over at night. I was now giving my nocturnal roommates an eviction notice. The Italian crew and cast were coming over for a Welcome to New York Party that night, and this was one aspect of the city I didn't want them to see. At least not at my place. As Romans, they were familiar with drugs and crime. Roaches no.

The thought of the party made me groan out loud. I had food orders to place, shopping, cleaning, chopping, some cooking to do, plus work with Massimo later in the afternoon. While lamenting the situation I'd placed myself in, I almost poured boric acid in my coffee. Why, I don't know. I had given up sugar years ago. A cold shower stung me to a waking state. After dressing quickly, I went shopping in the neighborhood for typical New York food: fried chicken, hummus, guacamole, nachos, egg rolls, sushi, bagels, strudel, and ice cream. Even though I meant to show off how international New York was, I was leaving out Italian food since the crew had just flown in from Rome seventy-two hours earlier.

When I got back to the apartment, I banged my broom against the ceiling to wake up Toni. Tania, my upstairs neighbor, had gone off to Japan for a month and asked me to watch over her one-bedroom apartment, giving me permission to use it if needed. After Toni complained about being cooped up in a small noisy hotel in the theater district with the rest of the crew, I offered him the keys.

Toni stood on the fire escape, popping his head through the open window. He sniffed loudly and kissed his fingers. *"Ti adoro!"* I was cooking his favorite food: eggs, bacon, sausage, and butter-dripping rye toast.

"Best hotel in New York City," Toni said, climbing through the window without difficulty despite his size.

"Do you ever think of using the door?" I asked, blowing him a kiss. He'd been scampering up and down the fire escape like a squirrel since he'd gotten here.

"Doors we have in Italy, fire escapes no. *Buon giorno,*" he said crossing the room to kiss me on both cheeks.

"Someone's going to mistake you for a thief." I handed him a heaping plate. "Here are the two-thousand calories you asked for."

He took the plate back across the room and leaned against the windowsill. *"Divino,"* he sighed after a few mouthfuls.

"How about a paper with breakfast?" I picked up the *Post* which I'd just bought and showed him the front page.

JO JUICED, it read. Underneath was a picture of Johanna in a white, low-cut evening dress, being helped out of a white limo by Diego. Behind the back seat window, Sara's face masked in elaborate rhinestone sunglasses peeked at the camera.

Toni frowned at the headline. "Juiced?"

"Wired, zinged, zapped," I said, showing off my limited knowledge of American slang. "ZZZZZZZZ," I added, shaking all over.

Toni shook his head. "She's fine today," he muttered, a piece of toast between his teeth. I raised one eyebrow. "She asked me to give her a wake-up call."

"Are you that close?"

Toni pushed his mouth to one side and didn't answer right away. For a moment, I thought his tongue was working something out from between his teeth. He made a noise, a closemouthed croak, which I took as a yes because of the way his eyes smiled.

"She's being interviewed by Barbara Walters this afternoon." Toni's eyes always gave him away.

"You're in love with her."

He gave me the coy grin of a kid caught with forbidden chocolate all over his chin. Which I translated to mean she loved him back. He looked that happy.

"But I thought . . ." I said, remembering how Massimo and Johanna had walked away last night, their bodies touching.

"That she and Massimo were *uno?*" Toni asked. "No, no, publicity. Pure publicity invented by Sara and Diego. Massimo's always dumping women anyway." He popped the last of the toast in his mouth. "No, Johanna loves me," he mumbled between crunches, putting the empty plate down on the fire escape. "But shhhh." A finger pressed against Toni's shiny lips. "The silence of the tomb, eh? No one must know. For the sake of the film."

"To hell with the film," I said, hugging and kissing

27

him. "Tell the world. I think it's great."

Toni, who was thirty-eight, had been looking for Lady Right for a long time. While I was waiting for my divorce—a very long process in Italy—there'd been a week when we thought we had found each other, but then we'd both realized it was simply desperate need. Thank God, that week had not ruined our friendship.

I sat down on the floor, pulling Toni down with me. "Johanna really loves you? You're sure?"

"You think she's too beautiful, too famous for me."

"I don't care what she is, does she love you?"

"Yes, yes, it happened before we started shooting. We'd known each other about three weeks. I went out to the villa she had rented on the Appian Way to take some more publicity shots. It was one of those Roman afternoons when the sun bursts like a crushed orange. You remember those, don't you, Sim? The heat, the stillness. I had her lie on a chaise longue under the wisteria, dressed in white. White softens her face, makes her skin glow. I leaned over to push back a lock of hair from her face, and she grabbed my wrist and told me she loved me. We made love right there with purple petals falling down on us." Toni put an arm around me and pulled me close.

"It was the most beautiful hour of my life. And now that hour's stretched out over a month." There was a moment of silence while I felt his chin bore into my scalp.

"Sim." He turned me around, his arms still holding me. "I want you to be as happy as I am."

Tall order, judging by the glow of his face. "Oh, I will be," I said, wiggling out of his embrace. "It's a little harder in New York. The sun's hidden by haze and soot, and stillness comes between the wails of sirens and car alarms."

I was making excuses. New York was as good a place to fall in love as Rome, especially in the fall, but my love life was a mess at that moment. I'd been dating Stan Greenhouse for over a year. I was pretty sure I was in love with him, but in the past three months he'd been slowly slipping away. I hadn't heard from him in two weeks, and I'd told myself that picking up the phone was in no way part of my Italian upbringing. To be honest, I was petrified of being rejected.

"You're the best, Toni," I said, ruffling his red hair. "I hope she is too."

For some reason I wasn't convinced she was. Toni was right, I did think her too beautiful, too famous to fall in love with my red-headed, loyal Sicilian friend. Or maybe it was plain jealousy. I got on my feet.

"We've got some cleaning up to do, and you promised to help."

Sissignore! Toni said, jumping to attention. I handed him the vacuum cleaner.

"Upstairs, while I clean veggies and mix the dip. At five, I've got to run to Massimo's hotel to go over tomorrow's scene."

"Where are we shooting?"

I took vegetables and sour cream out of my small refrigerator. "In Spanish Harlem."

Toni brought his dirty plate over, quickly washed it and dried it. "Is Johanna in that scene?"

"Don't you read the script? She's lurking across the street, taking pictures." I mixed Knorr dried vegetable soup with the sour cream and put it aside for the flavors to steep into the cream. "Too bad she's not coming to the party."

At the window Toni picked up the vacuum cleaner and headed up the fire escape. "She needs a night off."

"You'd better be here tonight," I called out as

29

I turned the water on at the kitchen sink. "I'm counting on you, Toni. And don't you dare eat another thing." He had put a two-pound bag of nachos under his arm just before slipping out the window.

"You'll croak of a heart attack."

"Don't get American on me!" Toni yelled back.

I stopped scraping carrots and thought about that. I *was* becoming American. I'd stopped smoking; I'd lost ten pounds ("your sexy Italian pounds" Sara had remarked with her natural bluntness); I was eating healthily; I'd bought a VCR to do body basics with Kathy Smith every day. I even owned four pairs of blue jeans (which I still hadn't worn because of my big butt) and one pair of Nikes (used only for aerobics). Then I thought of Massimo making fun of Americans last night. "Go, go, go," he had said. Why not?

I dried off my hands and dialed the Thirteenth Precinct. A voice slurred with boredom informed me Greenhouse was out on a job with his partner Raf. I left a message inviting Greenhouse to the party, adding on an afterthought that Johanna Gayle was coming. A wolf's whistle pierced my eardrum in response. I realize lying isn't a very American trait, but as a notorious Italian once said, if it gets you what you want, and what you want is good, then it's OK. Greenhouse was definitely good, if not excellent. Besides, Johanna just might show up.

Later, as I got out of my slacks and into a skirt for my meeting with Massimo, I tried not to worry about the job those two homicide detectives were on, about the possibility they might get killed. I mentally sent them a prayer and then thought how my relationship with Greenhouse seemed to be dying its own natural death. I checked the bathroom mirror: jaw-length thick brown hair curling around a pleasant face that bordered on attractive when a smile was added. I smiled and was reminded that at thirty-six my wrinkle-proof warranty had run out. I spread some concealer under my eyes. "Damn him," I told the ravishing creature in front of me, "I'm going to put up a fight that even Rocky couldn't beat."

A young doorman dressed in a somber imitation Yohji Yamamoto outfit opened the gleaming cherry mahogany doors of the Royalton Hotel on Forty-fourth Street. I headed right to the Round Bar, a cylindrical room so small it made my apartment feel like Grand Central. As I stepped inside, Massimo unfolded himself into a standing position and buttoned his double-breasted beige linen jacket under which he wore a charcoal gray turtleneck and roomy, front-pleated matching slacks. He wore ties only on screen.

"*Ciao*, Simona," he said and kissed me on both cheeks. "Champagne? Vodka? That's all they offer," he said in Italian. "If you're hungry, there's caviar." An open bottle of champagne was nesting in a chrome bucket next to Massimo's round, mirrored table. There was no one in the room, not even a bartender.

"We are to speak only in English, Massimo, and no thanks. If I drink alcohol, I'll start slurring words and you'll learn nothing." I would have loved to say "bring on a bucket of caviar" but for reasons of politeness didn't. Feeling virtuous, I sat down on a strange-looking square chair draped in a cotton dustcover that probably cost a fortune. The horned chrome back of the chair reached halfway up my spine and was ready to gouge me if I relaxed, which was another good reason not to eat or drink. The Royalton had been renovated a couple of years back by the French designer

Philippe Starck, and the hotel had become the chic place to stay for the European crowd. Sara and Diego were staying there too. Johanna was staying in her apartment on Central Park West.

"English comes easy to you," Massimo grumbled in his soft voice. "You have studied here."

I opened up the script to SCENE 7. INTERIOR. DAY.

"You look like a bum," I said, reading the part of an African-American undercover man who needs the prime minister's help.

"Siiimona," Massimo protested, his arm sweeping to one side. *"Un momento,* please. We are humans, not machines." His voice was muffled by the light gray-blue velvet padding that covered the circular walls and the banquettes and made the room look like a cell for the insanely rich.

"Massimo, you've got a lot of dialogue tomorrow, and I'm giving a party at nine o'clock tonight."

Massimo lifted his champagne flute and gave me his signature smile as if it were a blessing. "Yo, I'm groovy, man," he said, giving me the right script lines. I raised my thumb in approval.

"Groovy's dead," I read from the script, trying to get the required belligerent tone in my voice, "and don't 'yo' me. I graduated *cum laude* from Harvard."

"Forgive me, I vas trrying to assimilate your language." He said the lines without inflection. He wasn't going to waste any acting energy on me.

"Wah, wah, not va. And soften the 'r' in trying. And the 'g,' pretend it's not there."

"Simona, what does it matter? I have to dub it in later." Massimo lifted his eyelids and looked at me. His eyes were the watered-down color of decaf coffee.

"You might as well get it right from the start," I said. He shrugged and leaned back against the plush velvet banquette. I wondered why he always discarded his women. He didn't have the swagger of the gigolo. What came across off the screen was a lazy, almost homey charm. After he had left a well-known French actress a couple of years ago, he had mouthed his way through one bad film after another, almost ruining his career. This movie was going to bring him back, according to Sara. She and Massimo had been friends since the days when Sara had made him and herself famous with her second film, a slashing, bitter critique of the Roman Catholic Church's repression of women. Massimo had played a womanizing priest. I hoped she was right about his career getting back on track. There was a little-boy quality about Massimo that instinctively made me want to cheer him on.

We continued working, plowing through the scene several times. For once Massimo knew his lines well, tripping up only on the dreaded "th," and stopping to take a few sips of champagne. I avoided looking at his face even though I was aware of his gentle sensuality by the rustle of his clothes, the graceful movements of his hands. I wasn't attracted to him personally, but he made me think of Greenhouse, made me aware of the weight of his absence.

"Good work, eh, Simona?" Massimo said after we finished. He turned the champagne bottle over to drown in melted ice. "Say 'bravo, Massimo.' " He spoke with his eyes on my lips as if my answer was of vital importance to him. I found it disconcerting.

"Yes, very good," I said briskly, closing up the script and gathering various bits of paper, shopping lists, and the like that I invariably have with me.

"Simona, always on duty!" Sara Varni said in Italian, striding in with her lizard boots.

"No, the English lesson is over," Massimo said, happy to revert to the fluency of his own language.

Sara chucked me under the chin. "You look pretty

33

today." She was wearing a stretch black mini skirt over black tights and a mango yellow bowling shirt with VARNI stitched in raspberry (food colors were the advertising rage) over her left breast. The sunglasses *du jour* were two yawning lion's heads that covered most of her forehead and jutted out from her temples.

She leaned over me and kissed Massimo's forehead. He hadn't bothered to get up for her, and I wondered if it was because she was a longtime buddy or because she resembled a feisty, punky boy. A rather old boy, that is. Sara was Massimo's age; fifty-one.

"I hope you're not falling in love with Massimo," Sara said, curling herself up on the banquette next to him. As she turned, I saw VARNI, THE WINNING TEAM, stitched across her wide back. She lifted the wet champagne bottle and let it drip on the black-and-white tile floor. "He's under contract to Miss Gayle Goose. Where's a bartender? I want some pepper vodka."

"Don't call her that," Massimo said, the tone of his voice already admitting defeat.

"She's always squawking." Sara threw the bottle back in the bucket with an angry thrust that would have capsized the bucket if Massimo hadn't quickly reached to steady it. It was the first fast movement I'd seen him make since I'd known him. Was he as annoyed as I was?

"I thought the Gayle–Marini affair was a publicity stunt to promote the movie," I said, getting up to leave. I wasn't very happy at the thought of Johanna using Toni, maybe just to get some prettier shots of herself.

Sara grabbed my wrist. "It's an obsession, that's what it is. Sit down, don't run away. We've missed you back in Rome." Diego appeared in the doorway.

"Ah, *amore!*" Sara shrugged her bony, muscular

shoulders. "There's no bartender here."

Looking dignified in a navy-blue double-breasted suit, Diego stepped on the sunken spotlight in the center of the floor. "The bar doesn't open for another half hour." In that padded cell he looked bigger, calm, and capable. Watching him look at his wife with a quizzical smile of patience, I could see why Sara was so dependent on him. He was calm caretaker to her irrational genius, directing her explosive energy, giving her a base to come home to. And he obviously enjoyed being the hub of the wheel. How nice for them, I thought, Greenhouse slipping into my head.

"*Stolichnaya?*" Diego asked.

"*Si, amore,* the pepper kind. I love you." She blew him back a kiss and then tugged at her short, jagged-cut hair, heavily streaked to hide the gray. Around Diego, Sara softened, let herself be a woman. "Obsessions. Massimo and I have made them our life's work. Violence, hate, rape, feeding off love, integral to it. I am obsessed with Diego and film. Diego is obsessed with film and his family. Massimo is obsessed with Johanna and film." She took out a blue pack of Gauloises from her breast pocket and lit one, steeping the air with its black, foul smell. Sara was abrasive, self-centered, rude, prone to melodramatic exaggerations. And yet I liked her because of her creative intensity, her honesty, her need to express the ugly side of life so that we would see it and deal with it. The year before she had made a devastating film on AIDS that was praised at all the film festivals but that major distributors had categorically refused as too crude.

"Are you and Johanna really *uno?*" I asked Massimo, inadvertently picking up Toni's expression.

"We're going to marry New Year's Eve. In Venice."

"That is not for the press or anyone's ears, *capito?*" Sara said. "We are orchestrating the information so

35

that the media gets it bit by bit to stretch out the interest as long as possible." She took off her lions glasses and looked at me with small, squinting eyes. "We might as well use it since it's going to happen." She didn't look pleased. Without her glasses, she looked diminished, an aging woman with black pencil messily streaked across her eyelids. "I want to know who changed Johanna's lines last night?"

"Not me," I said. "I thought they were good."

"I want to know who gave them to her."

"She's not stupid," Massimo protested. "She thought them up herself."

Sara slipped her yawning lions back over her eyes. "Obsessions are energizing, Massimino," she said, cupping his chin with one hand, "but they're also blinding."

Diego walked back in the Round Bar holding three thin iced vodka glasses and the bottle of *Stolichnaya* under his arm. He frowned at Sara, and she stubbed out her cigarette.

"We were talking about obsessions," Sara said, unfolding her legs from the banquette so that Diego could sit next to her. He distributed glasses and joined her.

"So I overheard," Diego said as he poured. "I wish to state once and for all that I am no longer preoccupied with my family. They stopped thinking I married 'down' and they love you as their own. Your international fame has helped, of course."

Sara tapped Diego's cheek with the ice-cold glass. "Infamy, Diego. Fame is much too boring."

"Then perhaps I shouldn't have bought you this." He slipped a hand in his pocket and extracted a small pistol. "It's not loaded." Sara oohed and took it from him, caressing the mother-of-pearl handle.

"Is that supposed to keep the actors in line?" I

asked. Sara laughed.

"In New York," Diego said, "I am worried about Sara's vulnerability."

I didn't think Sara knew about vulnerabilities in any city. "Rome's not so safe," I suggested, sticking up for my adopted city.

"In Rome they may steal," Massimo said. "They don't kill." He reached across the table for Sara's pistol and pointed it at me. "And now we want to hear all about your passion. Simona's in love. She refuses to come back to Rome."

I, of course, had said nothing on the subject. At least not with words. I didn't know what my face was saying. My cheeks felt hot, which meant I was probably blushing. "My current obsession is to get back to my luxurious Greenwich Village apartment and get ready for the party." I got up and hooked my black Channel Thirteen bag on my shoulder like a true New Yorker. "Nine o'clock. You've got the address. Everybody coming?"

"Sicuro," Sara said and held up her hand for a high five salute in perfect American style.

There was no message from Greenhouse on the answering machine, and Toni was nowhere to be seen. That at least was a relief. I had no idea how to tell him about Johanna's wedding bells in a gondola. Toni had cleaned and straightened up both apartments and brightened them with clusters of purple asters. Flowers hadn't been in my budget and I mentally kissed him, wondering if it wasn't best to just keep my mouth shut. I couldn't bear the thought of hurting him.

They all arrived together with the usual Roman punctuality, at nine instead of eight: Sara, Diego, Massimo, the DP, the script girl, the assistant director, Massimo's makeup man, and Johanna's Hollywood makeup man. They clomped up the four flights, were amazed by the size of my apartment, quickly pounced on the food and wine, and then some of them wandered up the stairs to Tania's apartment. No Toni.

Sam walked up a few minutes after, his Rams cap firmly clasping his head. *"Evviva,"* I said, clapping my hands as Sam got his football girth through the door. Diego and Massimo shook his hand. Sam looked embarrassed.

Sara had curled herself on the windowsill, her upper face hidden by black glasses that spread out into thin spikes studded with rhinestones. They were the same mask-like glasses I had seen on the front page of the *Post*. The rest of her was covered in scarlet silk knickerbockers, opaque white silk stockings, gray satin ballerina flats, a gray cotton knit turtleneck, and a black leather motorcycle jacket. She fit right in with the Village.

"Do accidents come often on the American set?" Sara asked.

"No, we save 'em for big-time women directors." Sam took two giant steps to the fridge and got himself a beer. Sara slipped off the windowsill and strode over to him.

"Ehi, you are OK, Sam," she said, giving his chest half a hug. She loved it when people stood up to her. Sam raised his arms in surprise as if a much-feared cat had suddenly jumped in his lap. I wondered what made him so uncomfortable: women or just Sara.

I didn't stay in one place too long. I kept going up and down the stairs between Tania's apartment and mine, making sure everyone had something to drink, refilling plates with food. At one point, Diego asked me what the white powder along the kitchen counter was for, picking it up with his forefinger and sniffing it like cops do in the movies. Instead of answering, I admired his cashmere jacket and told him he was a genius at raising money.

"Sara's the genius," he said. "I simply have many acquaintances; although after our last fiasco it has not been easy."

"Getting Johanna Gayle was a real coup. Guarantees good American distribution."

Diego smiled. "If America believes in you, the rest of the world follows. At least in the world of cinema. She even attracted some Japanese money."

"Five million dollars is a lot of money for a female lead though." The movie business is no different from any other. The big money is reserved for actors only. "I hear Meryl Streep can't get more than three million."

Diego shrugged and declined the sushi I offered. By the look on his face, raw fish wasn't his thing. Or maybe it was the thought of the five million dollars that made him look a little sick.

From my tape deck, Lucio Dalla started singing that America was far away, on the other side of the moon. Sara beckoned Diego from a corner. He joined her and they hugged each other, pretending to dance. Massimo stood by the doorjamb, his hand over his mouth, a cigarette sticking out between his fingers, watching the crowded room.

I joined Sam on the landing for some air. He was looking down the stairwell gloomily.

"Is your assistant still in the hospital?" I asked as his big hand swept four tuna sushis from my plate.

"Yeah, Abe's OK, those medicos just like to poke

39

him a bit."

"You were great, Sam."

"It was Abe stickin' his hand in the fountain that saved her, not me. I never even fuckin' noticed the cable had moved."

"Moved?"

"Yeah, all those extras tripping over it, I guess."

I had noticed only two extras stumbling over the cable. Me and the man behind me. "Is that the only way it could have happened?" I asked.

He shook his head as he looked dawn the stairwell again. "Who would want to harm a beautiful thing like that?"

Johanna's blonde head was bobbing up the first flight of stairs with Toni right behind.

"Are you saying that somebody deliberately nicked that cable?" I asked, gripping Sam's arm. It felt like a tree trunk.

"No." Sam stepped back from the railing, still looking down. "I'm saying that Johanna Gayle is the most beautiful woman I've ever seen. I don't like people puttin' words in my mouth." I let go of his arm.

"See who I brought!" Toni yelled up, his freckled face splitting into a wonderful grin. Johanna wrapped one arm around him, waving the other at me. They looked like a happy couple, and I knew then I would never tell Toni about her Venice wedding plans.

"Look at her," Sam said, in a voice held low behind me. "She's got the breath of God on her." As she came closer, I did look: at her full oval face, the translucent skin, the dark, unplucked eyebrows, the small swollen mouth; at her gray-blue eyes flecked with brown as if they were beginning to rust. I sighed out loud. I didn't know about God's breath, but she sure had great genes. Why did Sam think anyone would want to harm her?

40

Johanna stepped up on the landing and saw Sam in the corner. "What the hell are you doing here?"

"I invited him," I said. "He saved your life, remember?"

"Get him out of here, Toni," Johanna said. "He's stalking me. He stands outside my building at night." She pulled at her T-shirt that kept slipping off one shoulder. "He tries to get a job in all my films. He's everywhere. I can't stand it!" Johanna started shaking.

Was she telling the truth? I looked at Sam, trying to understand what was going on. His face was impassive.

"You're out of your fuckin' mind," he said in his usual monotone voice. The landing creaked when he moved. Johanna winced. He walked past her, and halfway down the first flight, he turned back up with a pitying, sad look on his face. "You need help." Then he quickly walked down the four flights, the stairs sounding as if they were being splintered by his weight. When the front door slammed, Johanna slipped from behind Toni and smiled as if nothing had happened. She was either crazy or a very good actress.

"Hey, everybody," she called out as she turned toward the open door. "Thought I'd join you after all." Massimo walked over and kissed her cheeks. Diego and Sara stopped dancing.

"What was all that about?" I asked Toni sotto voce. "Did something happen between Sam and Johanna?"

"No, she's tired and nervous," Toni said. "She gets fussy. Purebreds are skittish, you know." He followed his love inside, sparing himself the "bullshit" I had on the tip of my tongue. I looked down the stairs and felt sorry for Sam.

"I just taped the best interview with Bawa." Johanna walked into the room in her tight Lauren jeans, bare shoulder still sticking out of the loose T-shirt. She paused, did a mannequin's half-turn on white alligator ankle boots, then took a tape out of a matching alligator satchel while Diego pushed the eject button on Dalla's croaky love words.

Toni slipped Johanna's tape into the VCR I'd just bought as part of an emergency kit to fill in for the missing Greenhouse; a kit also made up of a subscription to the Book-of-the-Month Club and a charge account at Ray's Pizza. I looked at my watch. It was now ten-thirty. I had the depressing feeling he wasn't going to show up.

Barbara Walters appeared in Johanna's all-white living room, dressed in a pink sweater and tan slacks. The left side of her face, the one Laurence Olivier had supposedly said was her best, faced the camera. "Johanna, we haven't met on television since . . ."

"Call everyone down," Diego said to me. "Johanna's going to talk about the film."

I ran upstairs, convinced the Roman crew to give up their fascination with American baseball (the TV was tuned to a Mets–Reds game), and stayed behind to clean up the mess.

When I came back down with a load of dirty dishes, the lights had been turned off, and the TV camera was closing in on a large silver-framed picture of an elegant gray-haired man in tweeds.

"Your father died three years ago," Barbara's voice said. "How devastating was his death?"

Camera shifted to Johanna turning one diamond stud earring round and round in her ear. "He'd always taken care of me. Mommy died when I was eight, so it was just him and me." Legs, sheathed in the same jeans she was wearing now, folded up onto the sofa. Her feet were bare. "I was . . ." She swallowed, and

42

the features of her face seemed to blur into a single emotion. This time she wasn't acting. Her father's death had hit her hard.

"This apartment belonged to your father. This is where you grew up. Aren't the memories overwhelming?"

Johanna's legs unfolded, moved to the other side of the sofa, and folded again, all with incredible grace. I was reminded of a swan folding its wings. But swans are faithful to their mates until death, I thought, looking over at Toni, sitting cross-legged on the floor. "I redecorated. White's my best color."

"So virginal I was afraid to contaminate the place." Sara said in a loud whisper meant to be heard. "I didn't put my ass down the whole time I was there."

Barbara moved to the edge of her armchair. Behind her, on the terrace, a red Japanese maple brushed against the glass repeatedly. "Tell me, Johanna, is it true that Massimo Marini is your first real love?" Quick cut to Johanna, the camera so close I could almost see the pores on her Maalox-white skin.

Toni shifted his legs and I cringed. I looked for Massimo. He had been sitting on the trunk I used as a coffee table. He wasn't there. In fact, he wasn't anywhere in the room. Neither was Johanna. I edged toward the open door. I hated Barbara Walters's question, I hated Toni not knowing about Venice, and I didn't like those two not being right there where we could all see them.

After getting no answer, Barbara changed to a more subtle tack. She folded her hands primly on her lap. "What's he like in bed?" The camera cut back to Johanna laughing her purring, throaty laugh, the one that endeared her to most of the men in the world.

"*People* magazine scooped you on that one, Barbara. I'm answering that very question tomorrow

43

night in an exclusive interview. That and a few other things."

Sara's trademark *"cazzo"* came out loud and clear. Her rhinestone glasses had fallen off and broken. Diego dutifully picked up the pieces, pocketed them, and handed her a replacement pair.

"She cannot think without them," he said to the party at large as if to excuse her for the interruption. On TV Johanna had finally let go of her earring. She was smiling.

I slipped out of the room and climbed the steps to Tania's. I had no business spying, but for some reason I'd got it into my head Johanna and Massimo were making love, and I wasn't going to allow that, not anywhere near Toni.

From the threshold of Tania's sparse dark bedroom, with its futon on the floor, a rice-paper screen against the window, a graceful aqua-blue vase reaching up from the bare wood floor, I looked at the light reflected in the long ebony-framed mirror. They were in the bathroom. Massimo was shaking her. All I could see of Johanna was her head thrown back, exposing a white gash of neck, and one bare, splotchy red shoulder. Massimo covered the rest of her.

"Why? Why? Why?" he whined with each shake. She groaned, stretching her neck back so much I thought it would snap.

Whatever was going on, I didn't like it. "Are you OK, Johanna?" I said, switching on the bedroom light. She tossed her head around, pushing Massimo away from her. He slowly faced the reflecting mirror. Looking calm, even a little sleepy, Massimo turned the bathroom light out and stepped into the room. He gave me his sad smile and lifted his palms upward in a gesture of helplessness. *"Siamo gelosi,"* he said, we are jealous, the "we" including me as a fellow Italian.

"That's no reason to shake her brains loose." Had Massimo found out about Toni? Tucking his arm into mine confidentially, Massimo tried to steer me away from the bedroom.

"Can I help?" I called out to Johanna. She closed the bathroom door. I followed Massimo out of Tania's apartment after I heard the toilet flush.

The interview was still going on when we got downstairs. A smiling Johanna was pushing her hands through her hair, pulling long strands away from her face.

"If you were a flower, what would you be?" Barbara asked.

"My father always gave me a gardenia. 'The most beautiful flower for the most beautiful girl.' He used to say that." She pulled one side of her T-shirt to cover a crescent of breast.

"If you touch gardenias, they bruise. Are you that delicate?"

Johanna opened her mouth and frowned like a child caught unprepared by the teacher. Then she shook her hair and shoulders. The T-shirt slid down, uncovering a shoulder, white flesh against white cotton becoming a soft curve of vulnerability.

"I want to be a weed," she said finally. "Nothing kills a weed." Her face froze in close-up. The interview was over.

Chapter Three

Greenhouse surprised me sometime in the middle of the night. I woke up to find a warm, naked, muscular body pressing against my back. I turned and pushed my nose into his chest to get the delicious smell of him. Without saying a word, I slipped on top of him. For a few delicious minutes, we kept it slow, teasing each other with kisses, licks, pinches. Then need got the best of us. Greenhouse lifted his hips and we danced together, sweating and softly calling out to each other until I froze and cried out as a thousand butterflies suddenly took flight inside me. Digging his hands into my hips, he let go with a moan.

"I see you got my message," I said after I rolled over and snuggled under his arm.

He kissed my forehead. "Now you can bring on Johanna Gayle."

"Too late. What time is it anyway?"

"Around three o'clock. I didn't get your message until I got back to the precinct at two."

"Ugly job?"

"No questions, Simona, please." Greenhouse had begun to divide his life into hermetically sealed compartments. His work, his son, his social life, the latter also divided so that I knew only what I witnessed.

46

When I asked to know more, he explained that he didn't like invasions.

"I'm surprised you got in the apartment," I said, feelings of resentments popping up quickly. "The key must be rusty by now." The soothing effect of his lovemaking wasn't lasting as long anymore. A sure sign of addiction.

He gave me a light kiss on the lips. "You've got the early morning grumps."

"No, I gave a party that started and ended with people growling at each other and I've missed you." I brushed my finger across his lips. "What's happening to us, honey?"

His hand brushed one breast, paused, then went back for a better touch. "Big Mamma," he said, cupping them both. I'm a little top heavy, an attribute Detective Greenhouse finds admirable.

"Come on, talk to me."

"Later." He squeezed and I squirmed.

"I've got to be at the Royalton at six-thirty this morning," I protested.

"Good, that gives us three more hours," Greenhouse said before slipping down toward my left nipple.

I suspected this was not the American way of fighting for a strong, healthy relationship, but how could I say no? I loved it.

At six-thirty in the morning Massimo had forgotten his lines, and my sleep-heavy head kept dropping to my chest. We rode up a deserted Madison Avenue in his plush silver limo; I tried to drill him, between bites of a bomb-sized bran muffin, widening my eyes to focus on the script page while he smoked his beloved

Muratti, droopy eyes glued to the PLEASE DO NOT SMOKE sign on the dashboard. After the first cigarette, the driver's eyes iced him from the rearview mirror.

"I will buy the car, OK?" Massimo told him and lit another Muratti. As the lighter reached his cigarette, his hand shook. During the night Massimo Marini had somehow lost his Mediterranean suavity. I had lost liters of sweat and all my sleep. The muffin was going to help me recuperate energy.

We stopped at a traffic light, and a silk charmeuse wedding gown flashed at me from Givenchy's corner window.

"Are you and Johanna really getting married?" I asked, imagining how beautiful Johanna would look in that simply cut gown. The only problem was that the groom wasn't going to be Toni.

"*Si, si, a Venezia,*" he snapped at me. "I already told you, no?" He sucked on his cigarette with puffy eyes closed. The car sped off, jerking me back into my seat. The wedding gown whisked away and so did Toni's dream.

By the time the chic boutiques of Madison Avenue had turned into the *bodegas* of Spanish Harlem, Massimo had barely mastered two lines for the day's shoot. Why he was so upset I couldn't begin to fathom. I knew I was going to have a hard day's work ahead of me so, on wobbly legs, I headed for the sticky sweet cheese Danish glistening on the food table.

Sara and the DP had set up the first shot of the day in front of a small abandoned building on 110th Street. The five-story brick structure was painted a bright turquoise on the first floor, then dark brick red. What made it movieworthy was the fire escape, completely covered with stuffed animals: giraffes, a lion, a horse, elephants, a donkey, a bald doll with one side of her face smeared with soot, lots of teddy bears, their necks tied to the rusty iron railing that zigzagged up the wall. The animals were tattered and dirty, some more than others depending on how long they'd been exposed to the "clean" New York air. On the last rung of the fire escape, at the very top, a brand-new panda stretched out enormous arms as if to hug us all.

"My contribution," Sara said, smiling below two red-white-and-blue rectangles, her American flag sunglasses. "These animals were put up there by the residents to claim their neighborhood for the children. No drugs they are saying. I like that."

I did too, I thought, looking up at those sooty, silent witnesses gazing across the street at the few trees of a housing project, wishing those animals had the magical power to hold off the drug tide that was flooding the city.

Toni climbed out of a window, camera hanging from his neck, and sat on the fire escape next to the hairless dirty-faced doll. He waved at me, a sandwich in his hand. In the other hand, he held McDonald's new paper package: his American breakfast. I blew him a kiss and tried to look as if nothing was wrong with the world. He snapped a picture of me, and I gave him the victory sign. He looked very tired, but then he hadn't come home last night.

After makeup, Massimo looked much more cheerful. His eyes were no longer puffy, and a thick layer of pancake hid those persistent night wrinkles that I was beginning to notice on my face too. He wrapped an arm around me and told me he couldn't live without me, which only meant he needed to be fed most of his lines.

The first scene was shot quickly. The prime minister, dressed in faded jeans, a gray sweatshirt, and dirty Reeboks so as to blend with the city, walked to the building, looked around to see if he was being followed, then slipped through the metal front door, shutting it behind him. The camera zoomed into the *Attencion — Mantenga este Porton Cerrado* sign on the door, and Sara yelled a gleeful "cut" over the drilling sounds of a construction site on the other side of Madison. She was especially happy because at the beginning of the shot, just before Massimo walked into frame, a pigeon had roosted on top of the doll hanging above him.

"E' simbolico," she said above the sound of bricks being spilled onto a truck bed. Symbolic of what I had no idea and didn't ask. She'd probably go on about the doll representing mankind tied down to the stairway of life and the pigeon standing in as man's soul or some such nonsense. With two very noisy takes, we were done.

The next scene was going to be shot in a large dusty room with graffiti on the walls. Empty vials of crack and discarded syringes had been placed in strategic points so that the camera could pick them up without having to close in on the detail. Sara wanted to be subtle. On one wall she'd asked the art director to paint a Keith Haring cartoon man with AIDS = DEATH underneath. That's subtle for Sara.

While the crew set up, I snatched another Danish and went to Massimo's van to work on his lines. As we drank from a thermos of black Italian espresso and I gorged myself, some of Massimo's memory came back. My brain, thanks to the calories, shifted from park to first.

Massimo sat back in his armchair and read from

the script. "What's your size?" It was the last line of the scene.

"Massimo, you can't pronounce the 'w' like a 'v.' It's a soft sound. Wa. If you can't get it just move your lips as if you were blowing Johanna a kiss. We'll worry about it in the dubbing studio."

"Why? Why? Why?" He threw the script against the wall and closed his eyes.

The same words he had used in the bathroom while shaking Johanna. "Who's making you jealous, Massimo?" I think I wanted to hear him say "Toni," as if that would legitimize Toni's affair, make his love for Johanna mean something.

Massimo lifted his eyelids slowly, exposing the watered-down color of his eyes. "I'm not a jealous man." He bent down and tapped the script three times before picking it up from the floor. It was an old theater superstition. "Please, I need to concentrate alone," he said. I had no choice but to step out into the sunny day unsatisfied.

I looked for Toni; one of the grips (workers who do the manual labor on a set) told me he had gone over to the construction site to take pictures. Across Madison, on the northwest corner, men in yellow hard hats signaled each other on top of a flat roof. Below them, Toni craned his neck back and clicked away.

It was nice to see something being fixed in that rundown area, I thought, as I climbed up the filthy, dark stairs of the teddy bear building. On the second floor, Sara and the DP were in a preshoot huddle, and Sam had finished setting up the lights.

"We missed you at the party," I told him. "You shouldn't have left."

"I'm not good with a crowd," Sam said, doing his leave-me-alone routine by showing me his back. I

51

gawked at the breadth of it and gave up.

In a corner, the African-American actor was working his shoulders and shaking his hands, preparing for the scene.

"You okay on your lines?" I asked. He gave me a thumbs-up sign and continued his relaxation exercises. I sat cross-legged next to the camera and prepared for one of those endless waits that are part of moviemaking.

Lights. Sound. Camera. Action.

SCENE 7. INT.
SPANISH HARLEM. DAY.

PRIME MINISTER walks in, looks around the dirty, bleak room, notices the vials and the syringes, the AIDS graffiti on the wall. SPECIAL AGENT JONES stands by an empty doorway.

PRIME MINISTER
(speaking with a touch of pompousness to indicate mistrust)
What is it you want from me?

SPECIAL AGENT JONES
A special interest group wants to make a simultaneous assassination attempt against the President of the United States and the top European leaders.
(He pushes steel-rimmed glasses against his nose.)
We need your help.

PRIME MINISTER
What special interest??

52

SPECIAL AGENT JONES

People are getting angrier and angrier. In the name of good causes too. Look at the pro-lifers, the animal protection groups, the environmentalists, the gay rights people. Spraying paint, screaming, shoving. It's very easy to step over the line.

CAMERA follows SPECIAL AGENT JONES's slow confident walk around the room. He goes to the window, tall and handsome in his dark gray, three-piece suit, a Brooks Brothers' club tie barely breaking the severity of his look. The stuffed tiger and the bald head of the doll hanging on the fire escape are visible through the broken pane glass. SPECIAL AGENT JONES looks back at PRIME MINISTER who pulls at his sweatshirt. He is meant to look awkward in his pseudo-American clothes.

SPECIAL AGENT JONES

According to our source, not everyone will be killed. The less aggressive leaders will get maimed. War begets war is what they're out to prove.

PRIME MINISTER

patiently
  Who is 'they'?

SPECIAL AGENT JONES

(kicking a broken vial from underfoot and speaking quickly, smoothly)
  The wounded of this war, of Nam, mothers, fathers, daughters, husbands, wives of the

dead. Pacifists. They've formed a secret organization to put a stop to war.

PRIME MINISTER
(struggles to take out a cigarette from the back pocket of his jeans. It comes out broken.)
What happened to marching and chanting slogans?

SPECIAL AGENT JONES
(takes out one of his own cigarettes from inside breast pocket, offers it to PRIME MINISTER who takes it. JONES lights his ZIPPO and brushes the flame against PRIME MINISTER's right hand.)
Pain gets heard better.

Burning Michele's hand — he'd put a protective salve on so he didn't get hurt — was another signature Sara Varni subtlety, like cutting to an egg breaking when the young protagonist of her first film lost her virginity. They were the kind of touches that kept Cinema d'Essai critics gurgling with glee or bile depending on the mood of the moment.

PRIME MINISTER
(sucking on his burnt palm)
Am I in danger?

SPECIAL AGENT JONES
Don't think so. Italy isn't much on war, is it? Cars, food and furniture are more your line. Some neat clothes too. Got my hands on a Versace jacket once. Sweet, but not exactly CIA.

54

(buttons the top two buttons of his jacket and
shakes one arm so the sleeve drops down to cover
most of his white shirt cuff.)

Across the street they kept up the drilling. I winked
at the sound man perched with his equipment on a
torn Formica counter in what had once been the
kitchen alcove. He tapped his earphones and
shrugged. I went back to lipreading to see if the two
actors slipped up on a line. The American was syllable perfect, and Massimo, to my complete surprise,
was doing beautifully. Except for his 'w's.' I'd given up
on those.

A bright sheet of sunlight decided to drop into that
bleary room. I relaxed, momentarily forgetting about
Toni and Johanna, and the absurdity of violence that
Sara was trying to portray with her film. I basked in
my easy moonlighting job, enjoying my full stomach
and the memory of Greenhouse's lovemaking.

PRIME MINISTER
(He stretches himself next to the taller American,
his face impassive)
    Why are you telling me about this group.
    What can I do? Design the uniforms?

SPECIAL AGENT JONES
(slowly takes off his glasses and licks his lips, sa-
voring the moment)

Long pause.

SPECIAL AGENT JONES
The Red Brigades, a nice Italian terrorist
group. That's who these guys have con-
tracted for the job in Europe. We thought

55

these terrorists were history, which shows we don't know anything. That's where you come in. You've been fighting them for years. You probably know what size underwear they got on.

(spreads out his hand in front of him with sudden force)

If you help, you'll be Prime Minister for life.

PRIME MINISTER
(takes the offered hand with his left, unburnt hand and smiles)

I'll get my tailor on it right away. What's your size?

This time the "w" was a barely exhaled kiss.

"Cut," Sara yelled. She was beaming. *"Bravi, bravi."*

Massimo slid eyes in my direction. "Good, eh? Spoken like a real *americano?"*

"Goodissimo!" I blew him a loud kiss.

"One more, please," Sara called out. "Jerry, the glasses from your face, not so slow, eh?" She wasn't going to let him get away with sneaking a scene from her Massimo.

Johanna and Diego came after lunch. Toni rushed over to greet her with a ham and Swiss on rye in one hand. She acknowledged him with a toss of blond hair, then she disappeared into her Winnebago. He looked crestfallen. I linked my arm in his and made small talk. Diego, looking relaxed in the same cashmere blazer I'd admired the night before, greeted us with nods and smiles. He kissed Sara on both cheeks and walked her away, arm around her waist, free hand gesticulating in private conversation.

After lunch, the crew set up the camera and the lights facing the east side of the street. In the next shot Johanna would come out of a fenced-in parking lot next to the teddy bear building, run across the street, and hide behind one of the trees of the housing project. The camera would then close in to show her aiming her telephoto lens at the window where the prime minister and the agent were talking.

Sara had timed the shooting of this scene to coincide with the New Haven line running across the stone bridge above the street half a block away. She wanted to get Johanna running across while a train sped past in the other direction to point out the "futility of man's effort to subvert the inevitable thrust toward destruction." Her words, my translation. Lousy in any case. She was just making use of the old movie cliché that speeding trains symbolize male sexuality.

Well, she got her shot. The New Haven line was on time. Johanna silently did her bit in an oversized Armani green-gray jacket, taupe T-shirt and tights. Her hairdresser had tousled her hair with a hair dryer just before "action" was called out, giving her an I-mean-business-but-I'm-still-sexy look. Toni took many shots of the scene. Too many, I thought. Sara did one more take, without the hurtling train, just for safety, and called it a wrap.

Toni hurried to Johanna and asked her to pose for some stills against the turquoise wall of the teddy bear building. They walked away together while I made a date with Massimo to go over the next day's lines after dinner.

"*Sei una cagna in calore,*" Toni yelled. I turned

around. He was crouched in front of Johanna, doubled over as if in pain, his face brick red.

"What the hell does that mean?" Johanna asked, leaning against the turquoise wall, her voice deep and angry.

"A bitch in heat!"

She slapped Toni hard. The back of his head snapped to one side. Coolly, she peeled herself off the wall and walked to her waiting white Cadillac. We all watched in silence, even Sara. I ran to Toni, but a sharp "Simona" stopped me. The top half of Johanna's face stared at me above the partially rolled up window. "We have some lines to go over," she said almost sweetly. "Come to my place at six-thirty, the Majestic, 115 Central Park West, nineteenth floor." The tinted glass window slid up, shutting her from sight, and the white chariot glided away. I stood in the middle of the street and wondered what she wanted. She had no more lines to shoot.

"Don't go," Toni said in a low voice. The others were looking away discreetly, getting back to the business of wrapping up the day's work. Toni came next to me. I noticed his left cheek was still red from Johanna's slap.

"She'll tell you what she doesn't have the courage to tell me to my face." He looked dazed. "Last night we were happy, today she didn't even know me. *E' finito.* The end." His hand tightened over my wrist until it hurt. "Don't go, please, don't go!"

"Come on, if that's what she wants to tell me, why not get it over with? My not going won't change your relationship." Behind Toni, Massimo, now looking his sophisticated Italian self in an open blue linen shirt, gray slacks, and a makeup-free face, waited by his black limo. He was waiting for me to join him.

58

"Let's go home, Toni. I'll tell Massimo I'm taking a cab with you."

"No, I want to take photos. I will photograph all of New York." Toni dropped my wrist and walked away toward the construction site. I let him go, knowing it was his way of blowing off steam. When he had missed out on being the still photographer for Bertolucci on *"The Last Emperor,"* he had taken pictures of the more than three hundred churches in Rome in three days.

After I sat back in the plush seat of Massimo's limo, I realized I didn't want to go to Johanna's. What if she did use me as a bad news messenger. How was I going to tell Toni? Damn, double damn! Why did he have to fall in love with the impossible in the first place?

After the driver dropped Massimo at the Royalton on Forty-fourth Street, I asked him to take me to Thirty-eighth street and Ninth Avenue. He raised an eyebrow. I was going to a section of New York called Hell's Kitchen, once notorious for its terrorizing gangs run by men nicknamed "Dutch," "Mallet," "Stumpy," "Goo Goo." I'd first gone to the area on a weekend my first May in New York, to stuff my loneliness at the Ninth Avenue International Food Festival. I'd come away gratefully full and unharmed. Hell's Kitchen didn't scare me.

"I'm going to a gym where a friend of mine works out," I told him. Unless he was on a very difficult case, Greenhouse's daily routine included an hour at the gym, usually between five and six P.M. I wasn't sure he was going to be there, but I thought it was a good way to wile away the half hour before seeing Johanna.

"Anywhere you want," he answered. "Thanks by

59

the way." On the way down, I had convinced Massimo not to smoke.

The limo stopped in front of a gray, two-story building that housed Greenhouse's gym on the second floor. A new sign had been put over a window that covered the length of the building. MUSCLES TO GO flashed in red neon over flexing biceps. Below, on the ground floor, was a dusty spice store that sold international packaged food that looked like a cache stored since World War I. You had to blow on the label to see what you were buying, as if you'd picked up a vintage wine from Rothschild's cellar.

"Want me to wait?" the driver asked. I thanked him, said I was fine, and walked up the two flights of narrow steps, sniffing the sharp smell of cloves all the way. Greenhouse doesn't like surprises, but I needed to talk. I get very emotional, jump to conclusions, open my mouth at the wrong moments. Talking to Greenhouse, listening to his calm reasoning always helped. He maintained his words were useless, that I went right ahead and did my crazy things, like the time I stuck my nose in a murder in my office and nearly got killed for the trouble, but he was wrong. The fact that he was in my life, if only in a small way, gave me strength. I had someone to fall back on at crisis time. Maybe I relied on him too much, but he was a man who not only made love but listened. A rare virtue among the men I'd known.

I opened the door and was immediately wrapped in the warm, humid smell of sweat laced with cloves. The place may have had a brand-new sign outside, but it sure hadn't spruced up its interior. The large, long window was grimy; the mats thrown on the floor were old and ripped; the Nautilus machines in one corner looked like dusty skeletons of dinosaurs. Greenhouse swore by this place, said it had the best trainer in the city. His Puerto Rican partner had introduced him to the place. Raf, who was a great pal to both of us, had muscles instead of bones. Greenhouse, thank God, didn't plan to go that far. He used it to keep a flat belly and to sweat away the blood and gore he had to deal with every day.

He wasn't on the Nautilus machines nor among the group of men and women spread out on mats doing leg lifts to the rhythm of a sleek hot pink leg reaching up at an impossible ninety-degree angle. I glanced down the leg, along the back of the Playboy body, sucked in my stomach in a dumb attempt to improve myself, then did a double take when I reached the profile partially covered by long blonde hair.

"Johanna," I called out. She finished her set, six more leg lifts, then wound her leg back, turning herself around. It wasn't Johanna although she was almost as beautiful.

"Sorry, thought you were someone else," I said with a silly grin on my face. Several men had turned around, annoyed. I had broken up the rhythm of the session. Greenhouse, fully dressed, appeared from the saloon doors of the dressing room, a towel over his shoulder.

"Hey, Stan, how about a movie tonight? I owe you one." Hot Pink had leaped up and was running across the sixty-foot room toward her Stan, my Greenhouse. I ran too, down the stairs and out of there. Out in the sun, on the gray cement of Thirty-eighth Street strewn with black garbage bags, I cursed myself for being there and thought of Massimo's "We are jealous." Damn right I was, I thought, angry that I couldn't control it, that I was so unsure of myself. A window across the street told me it was time for "Happy

Hour—Ladies Welcome" in red lipstick. In the mood I was in, I wasn't sure of being a lady, but the words "Happy Hour" appealed. I crossed the street and slipped inside a cool, dark corridor of a bar that had the bitter smell of beer and stale smoke. I'll just wait for him to come down, I told myself, then I'll go over and say hello. I ordered a Coke.

"It costs as much as a drink," an old man warned me from his bar stool. He was scraggy and tall; his spindly legs touched the floor.

"It doesn't have quite the same effect," I answered.

"That's my point," he said, offering me his half-empty shot glass. Permanently curved over that bar stool, he looked like a wind-beaten bird on his last perch. I shook my head at the offer and glanced beyond his curved silhouette at the bright rectangle of the window. Who was I fooling? I knew I wasn't waiting in that gin mill for the chance to greet Greenhouse. I wanted to see if he was going off with Hot Pink so that I could stew for the rest of the evening, stewing being one of the crazy things I do despite the fact that I know it's a waste of time. I sipped my expensive Coke in a booth covered in torn Naugahyde the color of dried blood and told myself to relax. Greenhouse hadn't come out yet so that meant he was waiting for Hot Pink to change. So what? He wasn't married to me, hadn't said he loved me. We were both free.

I waited and listened to the old man, the only other customer, rant about a *Daily News* story, something about a girl shooting her father with his own gun. He held up the paper for the bartender to see under one of the three lights in the place, a caged extension lamp that made me think I was lost in a mine shaft. "KID POPS POP" took up the whole front page.

"Fuckin' your own kid is fuckin' sick. Makes you ashamed to be a man. The kid's only eight!"

I felt Coke rise back up in my throat, and I quickly took money out of my purse. "This should cover a few more drinks," I said to the bartender. I handed him a twenty-dollar bill and hurried out of there.

"Hey thanks, pal," the old man called after me.

I looked down the still sunny street. After what I'd just heard, even Hell's Kitchen looked clean. Hot Pink didn't seem to matter that much anymore.

It was time to go and face Johanna. Even if she didn't mention Toni, I was mad enough now to ask her what the hell was going on. There is only so much playing around with people's feelings allowed in my book. Johanna was way over the limit. Just as I turned the corner on Eighth Avenue, I saw Hot Pink's unmistakable blond head next to a shoulder I was very familiar with. Greenhouse was getting pretty close to that limit himself.

By the time I walked to the Majestic on Seventy-first and Central Park West, I was calmer and out of breath. I was now in the land of huge, old apartments, mostly built in the twenties and thirties, with views of the park, which was now, in late September, just preparing for its gold and copper autumn show. It was the time of year I loved best in New York, when the cooling air and the changing light made me think of possibilities waiting just around the corner, of the renewed energy winter always brought me. I took a deep, relaxing breath.

Looking up at the Majestic with its soaring twin towers, I noticed ropes hanging from the cantilevered corners marring the art deco beauty of the huge, thirty-two-story building. On the left tower, men wrapped in heavy coats and hard hats stood on a wooden platform that looked as though it could swing them over the top of the trees right across the park to Fifth Avenue. They were waterproofing the building, and I shuddered at the thought of one of those ropes breaking.

Johanna had left word with the doorman to let me in without first buzzing up. I was taken to the nineteenth floor by a polite older man in a gray uniform, who pretended not to notice that I was covered with plaster dust I'd picked up on the set. I hadn't noticed myself until I saw his repeated sideways glances. He waited until I'd stepped through the door Johanna had left ajar. I suppose he was making sure I wouldn't wander the building like some long-ago tenant ghost bent on seeking revenge on the landlord.

The foyer was bigger than my apartment, a white expanse covered with Johanna's movie posters. The carpet was thick and so starkly white I took my shoes off. Since Johanna had a staff that took care of her dirt, she hadn't bothered to be careful. Streaks of soot cut across the carpet toward a long corridor on the left. I called out but got no answer. I guessed the staff had left for the day. I could see a slice of gleaming white-tiled kitchen just to my right. It was so neat it looked unused. I called out again, less loudly, hoping to get a chance to look at this white golf course of an apartment. I mean, I lived in a thimble compared to this. I took a quick walk around the right section of the apartment: a kitchen large enough for thirty people, a laundry room for ten, a maid's room for four, and a dining room for sixty. This last room she obviously never used. There was a white plastic table that looked like an Elsa Peretti bean and that was it.

No chairs, no other furniture. Only a full-length gilt mirror at one end. Weird.

The living room was normal elegant. I'd seen part of it on the Barbara Walters special the night before. A few antiques placed in corners broke the monotony of all that white: white carpet, white sofas and armchairs, a gleaming white marble coffee table. The woman was obsessed with white. Even the geraniums peeking over the windowsill were white. I walked to the terrace door and looked at rich New York. Across the park Fifth Avenue glowed pink orange in the late afternoon sun. I could see the Plaza in the southwest corner, the Pierre on the other side of the street. Twenty blocks up, the Metropolitan Museum with its glassed-in addition that houses some of the most beautiful art in the world sat among the trees. The bandshell in the park reminded me of summer concerts. Nearby, a lake looked like a smoothly cut piece of green glass.

I turned back into the room. Next to me a Pembroke table held half a dozen photographs of Johanna at various ages. She was beautiful from the day she was born. Her small mouth grinned in her childhood photos, smirked self-consciously in her teens. As an adult, she either gave her best Hollywood smile, or she stared at the camera with black eyebrows knitted. In each photo, she was held by her father, a square-jawed man who was vaguely familiar. He looked powerful, unsmiling, with unflinching eyes aimed straight at the camera. In her earlier pictures, he held Johanna on his lap; in the last ones he claimed her with an arm flung over her shoulder like a scarf. He was dark, big boned, didn't look in the least like Johanna. I looked around the room for pictures of her mother but found none. I went back to the

Pembroke table and tried to think of where I had seen that face before. The corner of my eye caught the deep red leaves of the maple tree on the terrace wiping a corner windowpane. I remembered the Barbara Walters interview. Of course, that's where I had seen him, in a TV closeup, while Barbara asked Johanna, "How devastating was his death?"

"Johanna, it's Simona," I called out, suddenly finding the silence of the apartment creepy. Across the street, the Dakota loomed at me. I couldn't help thinking of John Lennon's murder and the witches' coven of *Rosemary's Baby*.

"Johanna, are you there?" I crossed the foyer and strode into the long corridor that led to the bedrooms. I passed a small white library, colored only by the book covers on the shelves and a blue-and-white needlepoint pillow assuring me that BLONDES HAVE MORE FUN. Having brown hair, I believed it.

I knocked at a closed door. I got no answer and knocked again. Opening the door, I saw an overturned chair near the opposite wall. I didn't wonder why it was overturned, just that it was a deep green damask, jarring after all that white. And I remember thinking that it was probably her father's chair, and she couldn't bring herself to change it.

Something glittered at me next to my foot. Johanna had dropped one of her diamond stud earrings.

"Johanna, are you in the bathroom?" I walked around the king-size bed covered with a white velvet comforter toward the open door of the dressing room. I could see her tortoiseshell brush on the corner of the dressing table.

My knees sagged when I finally saw her. Johanna was on the other side of the dressing room door, lying on her stomach in her glistening white bathrobe. Her face, pillowed by the thick white carpet, turned to look at the bed. Above the neck, she had turned the deep red of the maple tree. Her flecked blue eyes popped out, her swollen tongue hung from her open mouth. An inch away, a smear of pink lipstick stained the carpet, looking like a last kiss.

I stared, without moving, without thinking. Until I saw the long nail wrapped in copper wire at the back of her neck, sticking out between folds of blonde hair.

I ran to the library and dialed 911. The operator kept asking me if I was sure she was dead. Calmly I told her, "Yes, she is dead. Very dead. Garroted dead." Then I threw up all over the needlepoint pillow.

Chapter Four

Toni sat crouched on my windowsill, looking down the street at the triangle of fenced-in garden where once there had been a women's jail. I sat on the floor below him, holding onto his naked foot, while the sky turned from an elegant evening blue to a sleepless night black.

The police had kept me over two hours in Johanna's library, asking questions about everyone in the movie crew, where they could find them, did I know of any reason why anyone would want to kill . . . on and on. The detective in charge, a Sergeant Fittipaldi, showed no mercy and brought me back to the bedroom to reenact the discovery of the body. I asked him if he wanted me to throw up again too. He shrugged, wouldn't allow me to clean up the mess I had made, afraid I might wipe away some clue along with my vomit, and told me I was free to go. I called Sara from a pay phone on the street to tell her the news and asked her to leave Toni to me.

He was waiting for me on the fire escape, sitting cross-legged, immobile, a small red-haired Buddha between two pots of basil. From the look on my face, he saw that something was very wrong.

"It's over. Dream gone," he said in a flat voice.

"Toni, come in here," was all I could bring myself to say.

"It's so demeaning. Why couldn't she tell me herself she was through with me?"

I waited until he had crossed the windowsill to tell him. Without saying a word, he sat on the narrow sill and hugged his knees. He hadn't budged since. If it hadn't been for the changing color of the sky and the growing darkness in my room, I would have said no time had passed, that we were in the frozen frame of an ugly movie.

Then the phone began to ring. Massimo called about our missed appointment, then Sara, Diego, all of the Italian crew, Massimo again. Everyone curious, leaving stupid questions on the answering machine about what and how much I'd seen. "Isn't it terrible? She being so beautiful and all," the script girl gushed at one point, as if the death of the ugly was much more acceptable. I picked the phone up when Massimo called a third time, his voice hoarse with strong emotion, and told him I'd call him back. I unplugged my phone and went upstairs to Tania's. I couldn't face talking to Massimo, listening to his grief, in front of Toni. It would have felt like cheating on him just the way Johanna had.

Massimo wanted confirmation she was dead from someone who had actually seen her. I gave it to him.

"Strangled?"

"Yes."

He then asked me what the room looked like, all the details of my visit. "I have to picture it, you understand," he said, his voice low, controlled — his acting voice. "Then I can accept. Tell me, tell me everything

69

you saw. *Ti prego,* Simona." I told him where I found her, what she was wearing, mentioned the overturned chair. I left out the bulging eyes, the purple, swollen cheek, her tongue licking the carpet, the shiny copper leash. Let him picture her as the beautiful Johanna she had been. And let me forget that sight.

Massimo hung up without saying anything more, and I noticed that Tania's kitchen clock read 11:04 P.M. By now every TV news program in the vast American land was talking about Johanna's death. Massimo and anyone else who cared to listen would get all the gory details.

I walked down to my apartment and turned on the light. Toni, on his feet now, looked at me with pure anguish on his face.

"I called her a bitch in heat! A bitch in heat!" He started pacing the perimeter of the room, repeating, "Bitch in heat, bitch in heat," until it picked up the rhythm of his footsteps. I grabbed his arm.

"Stop it, Toni!" I threw my body against his and hugged him as hard as I could, wanting to take his breath away, to stop the litany of guilt.

"I shouldn't have let her go off by herself. I always took her home, remember? You've seen me take her home after a day's shoot. I always took her home." He was hugging me back, talking into my hair, his tears wet on my cheek. I started crying too.

I heard the downstairs buzzer. I untangled myself from Toni and warily asked who it was on the intercom, afraid it was the media.

It was the police. I buzzed them up.

"Guys, have a heart," I said from my tiny landing, looking down on a melon-shaped scalp half covered by a few carefully placed strands of black hair. "I've already told Sergeant Fittipaldi all I know at the Ma-

70

jestic."

I got no answer, just the sound of one set of heavy footsteps with a down beat of lighter ones coming from a second policeman, this one with a curly mop of blond hair that looked like cornflakes.

When they reached my landing, I said "Hi" with a smile, knowing they didn't like being there anymore than I liked it. Since I've known Greenhouse and his partner Raf, policemen didn't intimidate me, even when they look as nasty as Peeled Melon did.

He was over the regulation weight limit by at least fifteen pounds, and he hadn't liked walking up four flights. Hemorrhoids, acid stomach, corns, bad marriage, worse job were all there, eating at his face.

"We're not interested in you," he said, breaking each word with a loud intake of breath. "But a Toni Berto. We've been told he lives here." Corn Flakes, a nice-looking man with a wide, Hawaiian-print tie loudly pointing to his very trim stomach, raised a badge that I didn't bother to check up close.

I wondered if they had found out about Toni's relationship to Johanna. After that afternoon's outbreak, the whole set had to know he was in love with her, but that didn't necessarily mean anyone knew they were sleeping together.

"It's been a rough day for all of us," I said, deciding no one needed to find out that one particular fact. Not the police, not Massimo, and especially not the gossipy, mean-spirited movie world. "Can't this wait until tomorrow?"

"Nope," Peeled Melon said and peered through the door I'd left ajar.

Toni was in full view, sitting at the window, backlit by the street lamp just outside. He reminded me of one of those teddy bears propped up on the fire escape up in Spanish Harlem, tattered, dirty, the stuffing knocked out of him.

Peeled Melon walked in and introduced himself. Toni ignored him and continued to look out the window. Corn Flakes waited for me to walk in the apartment first, then stood by the door in silence, as polite and discreet as a butler.

"Mister Berto, where'd ya go after work today?" Peeled Melon asked in a small, high-pitched voice that was pure New York. Toni didn't answer. I told him in rapid Italian that they were just routine questions the police had to ask, and the faster the answers came, the faster they'd leave. Peeled Melon turned his head in my direction and glowered. I translated what I'd said.

"That's right. Routine. So where were you?"

"Vaffanculo!" Toni said under his breath.

"What's that?" Peeled Melon had moved in closer to the window. He was only about two feet from Toni, his stomach sagging over his pants like a ball of dough. "Wanna repeat that?" Toni shook his head.

"Hey, yer good with the insults. A fine, upright New York detective gets 'Up yer ass.' A gorgeous gal like Johanna Gayle's 'a bitch in heat.' Real nice."

Toni clenched a fist. Peeled Melon got closer.

"How 'bout tellin' us what yer were doin' in her apartment all night last night, how about telling us why'd yer try to shout yerself back in today?"

I looked at Toni in surprise. He hadn't said anything about being at the Majestic that afternoon.

"How 'bout tellin' us why she didn' want nothin' to do with yer, why the doorman had to get help to get yer outta there? How about tellin' us, huh?"

"I loved her!" Toni yelled, suddenly jumping up and shaking a fist in the air.

72

I rushed over to put a restraining arm around Toni's waist. If Peeled Melon didn't shut up, Toni wasn't going to limit himself to a Zsa Zsa slap.

"Sooo, she was gonna get hitched to the big actor." Something resembling a smile wiped itself across the detective's face. "Information confirmed by the butch director with the glasses, and by *People* magazine. *And* yer say yer loved 'er, but yer called her names in front of a whole gang of men. Why? Me, I'd a kept quiet. If the lady was a bitch in heat, seems to me it was all to yer advantage. That way yer got to bang her too."

Toni whipped out his fist, but Peeled Melon was faster. He caught Toni's wrists and held them in a steely grip while Corn Flakes stepped in between me and Toni. I heard the dry click of handcuffs being shut and the beginning words of the Miranda Act.

"Hey, come on, let's keep this in perspective," I protested. "Toni's upset. He'd never have taken a swing at you if you hadn't provoked him. Come on, enough's enough. Take those cuffs off him." Only Corn Flakes was paying attention. He kept looking at my hands moving in front of me as if I might make a mean grab any moment. I tried another tactic. "Listen, Stan Greenhouse and Raf Garcia over at the Thirteenth are really good friends of mine. So come on, how about a break here?"

Peeled Melon and Toni were out the door by then. All Greenhouse and Raf's names got me was the courtesy of a withering look. Corn Flakes was kinder. "We've got to take him down for questioning."

Peeled Melon trundled down the stairs with Toni in tow. I ran after them.

"Why in the middle of the night? Can't this wait until morning? Can I come with him? His English isn't that good." I was like a worried mother, asking questions that got no answers, trying to touch Toni to reassure him and myself that everything was OK.

Peeled Melon opened the back door of an unmarked car parked in front of a fire hydrant.

"How long will it take?"

"Maybe two years if I book him for takin' a swing at me."

I gasped. From the back seat, Toni told me to go to sleep, and Corn Flakes gave me a thumbs-up sign. "Hey, I know Greenhouse," he said in a cheery voice. "He's an OK guy." The car took off.

I ran back upstairs and called the OK guy.

After many rings, the phone was finally picked up on the other end.

"They've just taken Toni. The rudest cop I've ever met insulted him, and Toni took a swing . . ."

"Who is this, please?" a small, sleepy voice asked.

"Oh, Willy, I'm sorry." His thirteen-year-old son had answered. I noticed that his voice had not begun to crack yet. Odd details creep in at unexpected times.

"Who is this, please?" So polite, I thought, with all those pleases. Frightened probably under that coat of sleepiness.

I took a deep breath. "Simona Griffo, a friend of your father's," I said, hating this awkward late-night introduction to the one person in Greenhouse's life I had been dying to meet.

"I've been trying to get you ever since I got word you found her." Greenhouse had grabbed the phone. "Where've you been? I would have come over but . . ."

"You had Willy." I couldn't begrudge him his son, but it still didn't make me feel good. "I'm fine. I'm worried about Toni. He nearly hit this detective . . ."

74

I went on and unloaded the whole story. As I'd said before, Greenhouse was good at listening. When I was through, he said he'd find out the name of the arresting cop and talk him out of pressing charges.

"That man was awful. He deserved a punch in the face." I had set in my mind that Toni had been taken away only because he had physically threatened a law enforcement officer. I refused to contemplate any other danger to Toni's freedom.

"The job doesn't exactly encourage human kindness."

"Toni will be all right?"

"I'll get on the phone right now. If he's clear, he'll be fine."

"Thanks, and tell Willy I'm sorry I woke him up."

"Are you sure you're all right?"

No, I want you over here, I want to lean against your back and forget today. Maybe talk about picnics in the park, envisioning you and Willy playing softball, being part of your family in some small way.

They were only thoughts.

"Call me back if you have some news," I said instead. Turning off the lights, I sat on the floor to wait.

Ten minutes later the phone rang.

"They picked him up for routine questioning. You'll have Toni back in the morning. They're not going to press any charges."

"Thanks a lot."

"Want me to come over for a few minutes?" His voice sounded warm, caring. "Willy's sound asleep."

I wanted him next to me more than anything. "Thanks for the offer. I'm fine." I thought I heard a sigh of relief. Greenhouse knew I wouldn't accept, not when Willy might wake up and find his father gone. You don't do that to a child who's gone through a divorce.

"I'll call you in the morning," Greenhouse said, ending with the sound of a kiss. I hung up the phone and stretched out on the rug, too wiped out to climb up the wooden ladder to my loft bed.

Chapter Five

The next morning there was no sign of Toni. His bed hadn't been slept in, and his camera was where he had left it the night before, perched on my TV set. I turned on the seven-thirty news on Channel Four to hear that hurricane Jezebel was threatening the Gulf of Mexico, and that several people were being questioned in the "gruesome murder of Hollywood's favorite blonde, Johanna Gayle."

"Several people," I liked the sound of that. Toni wasn't the only suspect.

I called Greenhouse at home while Willard Scott, *sans* toupee, showed off a trio of centenarians, all women. The phone rang and rang, and for a split second I saw myself at a hundred, sour, crotchety, brittle leg pulsing nervously, still waiting for Greenhouse to pick up.

Finally he answered. He'd been in the shower. Willy was still around but had suddenly become phone shy. My doing probably.

"Toni's not back," I said in a belligerent tone that accused Greenhouse of all the ills of the modern world.

There was a short pause while in the background Willy asked his father what shirt he should wear.

What normal thirteen-year-old asks a parent what to wear? Poor kid, he really did want to make contact.

"Look, I'm not getting any real information from the Twentieth," Greenhouse said, after telling Willy blue was the color of the day. "Orders from the top are to clam up. Johanna Gayle's murder is big news, every American eye is staring, waiting to see what happens next." He gulped, coffee probably, black instant, with a sprinkling of cinnamon, the way Irene, his ex, had always made it. After his first night over, I had dutifully bought a small jar of the spice even though I couldn't stand the smell or taste of it.

"There's a lot of pressure for a quick resolution," he said. "It'll be good publicity for New York City cops if they get the guy right away, especially after last week." A policeman had shot a pregnant black woman in Tompkins Square Park, thinking she was about to shoot him. Screaming angrily because a passerby had called her "vermin on the loose," she had reached in her purse for an envelope with her address on it to prove she wasn't homeless. The bullet had grazed her hip. With the shock she had lost the baby.

"Toni didn't kill Johanna."

"There's a rookie assistant D.A. who's developed an overnight case of acne he's so excited about this case. He wants his name in print badly enough to hang the wrong guy."

"You mean Toni?"

"At this point I don't know. Look, I have to drive Willy to school. I'll see what I can find out and call you back."

"If this is what justice amounts to, how can you stand being a cop?" I was suddenly angry at a way of life that churned the weak into mincemeat, even ashamed that it had never really hit me before how raw a deal some people got. Like that black woman sitting on the bench, minding her business, maybe deciding that having her fifth baby was really OK. Like that eight-year-old having to submit to the nauseating weight of her father's body on top of hers until she got hold of a loaded gun. Like lovely Johanna strangled into a purple puffball, with Toni maybe being accused of her murder now. Toni, my friend. It was that "my" that sensitized me, that connected me to those ugly realities and made me feel awful.

"I'm not always sure I can stand it," Greenhouse said in a weary tone. We had been through this before, mainly when I worried he was going to end up like a sieve passing blood. Maybe he'd been hearing it from his wife for many years. I knew he had many doubts about his work. He said he wanted to stay alive to watch Willy become a man, and that meant getting out of the force. But he had this strong loyalty to the police. His father had been killed in a mugging, and in a moment when he had wanted to scream himself into shards of anger and pain, he had been surrounded by policemen who were strong and friendly, who never broke under pressure. Their camaraderie had wooed him to abandon business school plans and join the force. "I try to be fair and I try to be safe."

"I hate it, I just hate it," I said, without really knowing what "it" was: Toni's arrest, Greenhouse's job, my loneliness, the overwhelming city.

"Listen, Simona, stay out of this one." He was worried, knowing my anger at "it" might make me want to move the events along myself. "Please, go make movies, find pretty models, cook a hundred meals if you feel itchy, but *don't* go sticking your Roman nose into this murder. You hear me? I've got to run or

Willy'll be late. I'll keep you posted."

No, I wasn't going to stay out of it. Toni needed help, and I was going to give it to him.

The day's shoot had been canceled, and I was free until five o'clock that afternoon when Diego had called a production meeting to which I was invited. I had lots of hours in which to stick my oversized "Roman nose" where I wanted: into Johanna Gayle's murder.

I got dressed in what I call my "10021 suit," 10021 being a posh zip code on the east side of New York, between Sixty-first Street and Eightieth, where supposedly the best and the richest live and shop. The suit is a gray-and-beige-striped Armani knock-off I had found in Rome at a bargain price, and I wear it whenever I want to impress and charm, mostly, new clients at the advertising agency where I normally work. I had a nice wrinkle-enhancing tan left over from the summer; I hadn't put on my winter layer of fat yet, so I looked pretty decent, I thought. Off I went to the Majestic, taking the subway from West Fourth Street. The scene of the crime seemed the logical place to start. I had no idea what information I might get, if any, that could be of help to Toni, but I certainly wasn't going to sit around cooking. A hundred meals indeed! I had the urge to get a cotton swab and clean out my ears. If Greenhouse hadn't been personally involved, he'd have probably told me to go and get laid.

I walked out of the subway at Seventy-second and Central Park West and wondered how the murderer had gotten into Johanna's apartment. Security was tight in expensive buildings. Fire stairs were kept locked from the outside, doormen watched your every move, the elevator was manned. I'd been watched until I entered Johanna's apartment. Toni had apparently tried to get in to see Johanna but had not succeeded. Peeled Melon had said something about the doorman calling for help to get Toni out of the building. I could imagine the scene, Toni squirming and screaming Italian obscenities, his red-haired head popping up like a ping pong ball in a rushing stream of gray uniforms. As I adjusted to the sudden sunlight of the outdoors, I spotted something red across the street, on the park side. Not red hair, but a bright red T-shirt filled with muscle and hard weight. It was Sam, gazing up at the Majestic, the top half of his face hidden by his baseball cap, his mouth hanging open, as if the Majestic were his first look at a wonder of the world. I called out his name and waved. He didn't start when he saw me. His football days were long over; his body was too heavy to make sudden movements. My presence made a difference though. I could tell even at that distance, from the way he stiffened to attention as if my voice had sprayed him with quick-drying cement. While I waited for the light to change, he turned around and walked away toward Strawberry Fields, Yoko Ono's memorial to John Lennon. I ran after him, dodging a Yellow Cab that honked for its right of way.

I lost him. I looked down the two available paths and saw no red shirt. Later, I realized he must have taken his shirt off, knowing I would be looking for the obvious.

I turned back toward the Majestic. The waterproofers were still there, and I wondered if they had seen anything, but then I noticed they were working many floors below Johanna's. She would have had to scream to be heard by them, and I didn't think the murderer had given her time for that. Whoever he was, he'd been somebody she knew. How else had he got in? The doorman would be able to tell me who'd been admitted that day, if he was willing. I'd even brought a hundred dollars with me to try the old movie bribe, although I doubted that would work. The Majestic probably employed old-fashioned doormen who were very loyal to their castle.

I was out of luck anyway. Not even a real Armani suit decked with Cartier jewelry would have gotten me a revealing chitchat with the doorman. A buzzing swarm of reporters clustered around a short man well into his seventies, bristling in his freshly ironed gray uniform in front of the entrance. Just in case the doorman remembered my face from yesterday, I put on my sunglasses, à la Garbo, and moved up closer to listen.

He was having a grand old time, not letting any of the reporters step inside, opening the door to the tenants and their guests with a sweep of his hat, all the while giving the history of the building, how it was built by Irwin S. Chanin to replace a luxury hotel in the middle of the Depression, how they'd had many an infamous tenant. Meyer Lansky had occupied 4F and had paid well. Lucky Luciano had lived in 16A for a few years. Whenever a reporter tried to bring the doorman to the more current event of Johanna's death, the man, with a friendly grin, would readjust his white-braided hat and say, "I cannot be telling you that," with a slight Irish lilt. As I walked away, I heard him brag of the assassination attempt against Frank Costello, well known to the staff even before the Kefauver Crime Commission investigation because he was so tight-fisted.

"Costello was a horse of a man. Both he and our entrance marble survived the bullet."

I walked to the Mayflower Hotel on Sixty-first Street and looked up Sam in a Manhattan phone book. He wasn't listed. What had he been doing in front of Johanna's apartment building? Was it simple curiosity? I remembered Johanna's paranoid reaction to Sam at my party and decided I wanted to know more about him. I called the apartment to find out if Greenhouse had left a message. After beeping three times into the phone, I gave up. Being mechanically retarded, I couldn't seem to learn how to work the answering machine from another phone. I called Tania's in case Toni was home. No answer.

At the Thirteenth Precinct I was told that Greenhouse and Raf were out on "that case." I pretended to know all about "that case" and left word for Greenhouse to call ASAP if he had news. Then I called the assistant director at the Broadway, the seedy hotel where the Italian crew was staying, hoping to get Sam Weston's telephone number. None of the crew was in. They were probably all scattered around the city stocking up on CDs and Timberland shoes, both much cheaper in this country.

I remembered the electricians' union, the National Association of Broadcast Employees and Technicians, and looked them up in the phone book. Nabet, as everyone in the movie industry calls them, was fairly close, West Fifty-sixth and Seventh Avenue, five short blocks down, one long one across. My heels would make it.

Nabet, "no ability, but everyone tries," Sam had said laughing on the first night of shooting. The receptionist I was looking at behind the glass partition of the union's office must have had a lot of ability. She sure wasn't trying, at least not with me. Three times I told her I was part of the crew of *Where Goes the Future?* and that Sam was the gaffer on the shoot, adding that I needed to get hold of him for a production meeting. I got no answer. Had she sensed my lie?

The receptionist sat in front of a PC, her long orange nails poised to tear out its microchip heart. Behind her was a view of the corn-colored Worldwide Plaza tower with its pyramid tip. The Hudson River and New Jersey acted as a flat blue-and-gray backdrop. The office, very neat and sunny, seemed a nice place to work, but I doubted the receptionist thought so. She couldn't have been more than twenty-five, and she might have been pretty if she ever unpuckered her face and released her dark hair, which she'd swept out at the temples into long curved wings stiff with hair spray. As it was, she looked embalmed in flight.

I leaned over to see what she was staring at and saw the cursor blink back at her under the word "prevaracation."

One of the advantages of learning English as a second language is good spelling. "Try an 'i' instead of the second 'a,' " I offered as a way to relax those orange-tipped claws.

With two sharp flicks, the change was made and she looked up, somewhere behind my shoulder. No smile of gratitude, though.

"Johanna Gayle's film," she said in a colorless tone.

"The very one."

"I've already been bugged by the police, reporters. Now you!" That "you" sounded as if I were by far the worst.

"Did they all want Sam's address?"

"List of all union members on the shoot, addresses, telephone numbers." She turned back to the PC.

"How about a little help with Sam's?"

"Help. That's what I wanna scream." She turned

around, her voice now colored with high, stretched out notes about to snap. "All I get day and night is 'how about doin this,' 'doin' that,' 'hey be a pal,' a little tap on the ass when they can sneak it in, 'gee, sorry about that, didn't mean nothin' by it,' so many taps my ass is startin' to shine." She straightened out her hands on the keyboard and looked at the length of her nails. She was at least proud of that achievement. "Nope, for three hundred a week, two kids and no husband, I help myself." Her voice had calmed down. "I got no time for you."

"Sorry you feel that way," I said and headed for the door. Not that I could blame her really.

"You sorry? In that suit?" She shook out her up-tilted wings. "I even had to take a four-hundred-dollar computer course to get this shit job. Three hundred a week for chrissakes, while Johanna Gayle got five million for six lousy weeks of work."

"Johanna Gayle got dead," I said and closed the door.

Outside on Seventh Avenue I felt better. There was a nice cool breeze that tickled my face. God, I hoped I never had to lead her life. I realized my Roman nose hadn't gotten hold of anything, so I decided to go home to wait for Toni and see if Greenhouse had called with any information. I would get Sam's address at the production meeting that night.

As I waited at the light to take the subway home at Columbus Circle, a man's voice called out, "Where goes the future?" I turned around to see one of Sam's electricians standing outside of the OTB office. He walked toward me, putting a racing form in his jeans' pocket.

"Hey, I just bet on a filly by the name of 'Killer Jo,' bound to win, whatta ya think?" He held up a thin, long hand in salute. "Sorry, don't know your name, but I recognized you as one of the crew. Isn't that somethin' about Johanna Gayle. I sure hope this doesn't mean we're outta a job. Oh, sorry, I'm Jerry and you're . . . ?"

"Simona."

Jerry wiped his flat stomach with a hand and hitched up his pants. He seemed to be having a hard time standing still.

"You wouldn't by chance have Sam's address and telephone number?" He gave it to me but warned me to call first. Sam didn't like surprises.

I thanked him and asked him if Abe had recovered from the electric shock he'd got at Lincoln Center.

Jerry laughed and shifted his weight back and forth on worn-out high tops, nervous like a horse at the starting gate. "Abe's great. He's gone off to Wyoming for a rest-up. There wasn't much wrong with him, his thumb barely touched the water, but it sure is a good excuse to collect disability."

"Where in Wyoming?"

The Seventh Avenue light turned yellow, and Jerry leaned forward. "Have no idea. In some stream, fishing. Real primitive, that's the way he likes it. Man, I bet he doesn't even know about the murder." WALK appeared across the street and Jerry was off. I followed.

"Why wouldn't he?"

"No electricity." He was walking fast, in the opposite direction from Columbus Circle.

"It's in all the papers."

"Yeah, that's right. Gotta run." He lifted his long hand again and took off. After a few steps, he did a half turn on the balls of his feet as nimbly as Larry Bird. "Hope we still got a shoot."

I raised my hands in the air and shrugged. I hadn't even thought of that possibility and didn't care. I wanted Toni back. I was going to cook him the most fattening breakfast ever, pancakes, bacon, sausages, hashed browns, steak: a hungry Italian man's dream of America.

My answering machine was blinking red. I pushed the playback button. Greenhouse, his voice soft with concern, informed me that Toni had been booked for Johanna's murder.

"God, I hate telling you this over the phone," he said, adding that he and Raf were going to be out all day so he couldn't come over.

The doormen and the elevator man hadn't seen Toni go upstairs, but his red hair had been found underneath Johanna's fingernails. That was all the information he had. Enough to put Toni on trial.

"Please stay put," he asked. "Let me see what I can do."

I went over to the refrigerator, took out a leftover bowl of vegetable dip, and started to eat, fingerful by fingerful. It was my usual response to bad news.

I sat on the floor, licking my finger and wondering if Greenhouse wasn't holding something back just to keep me out of it. It was possible. I finished the bowl and reached for the phone without bothering to wipe my finger clean, dialed the Royalton and asked for room 702. Diego answered after the first ring. He'd had the news from Toni directly and got the Italian consul general to step in.

"I want to see him," I said, beginning to blubber.

"Tomorrow. If they indict him today, you'll see him tomorrow. *Su, su,* I'm taking care of everything."

I was crying loudly now. Not just for Toni, I think, but for the whole ugly mess.

"*Calma,* Simona, the Consulate has suggested an excellent criminal lawyer from an established firm. This lawyer has agreed to represent Toni at my expense but has asked us not to interfere." Diego had developed a chilling, ruffled-feathers tone that dried my tears real fast.

" 'No hysterical Italians' is the diplomatic way the lawyer put it. I've convinced Sara to be patient. I suggest the same for you. The lawyer has assured me he's been successful even in the most doubtful cases."

"Damn it, Toni's not guilty!" I hung up at that point, washed my hands, and walked over to Balducci's, a posh Italian foodstore on the corner. I think better in the presence of neatly laid out peppers and eggplant. The smell of salami and prosciutto clears my sinuses and my brain. I looked at the mâche lettuce for $4.95 a pound and thought about the "accident" at Lincoln Center. It could easily have been a first attempt to kill Johanna, two hundred extras and a crew ready to testify it had been a terrible accident. Anyone with a basic knowledge of electricity could have cut the cable and pushed it against the fountain's drain valve.

I walked over to the freshly made ravioli stacked neatly against one wall, underneath the red, white, and green homemade pasta sauces, and wondered if Toni could possibly have killed Johanna. She'd been cruel to him, but he'd been used to that, always falling in love with a woman too beautiful or too ambitious to settle for a loving, mild man like him. He was a classic case of a smart man making foolish choices for some unclear need to be humiliated, a need usually attributed to women. I remembered Toni just two days ago, perched on my windowsill, stuffing his face with breakfast cholesterol, happiness gleaming on his face like suntan oil.

No, my sweet Toni couldn't have murdered Johanna, no matter how degraded he'd been made to feel. To twist wire into someone's neck took a contorted, sick strength I was sure he didn't have.

I went over to the bread counter and bought an Eli's sour dough onion baguette. If anything, Toni would have used a gun, to avoid direct contact with Johanna. He would have never been able to kill her once he'd touched her. "Her skin feels like cashmere," he had once told me with awe in his voice.

Outside, in front of the entrance to the New Jersey PATH train, a neatly dressed man stared at me blankly. As I walked past, munching on a bread end, the man whipped around and yelled obscenities at me. I hurried off afraid he would follow, afraid of his surprising, sudden hate of me. Between the man's violent words, I began to hear Toni's angry voice insulting Johanna.

God, was I doubting his innocence?

Sam. Sam was the man I had to see, I told myself as I waited in a doorway for the man to shut up. Sam, who had been the only one to see the cut cable—Sam, who had frightened Johanna—Sam, who had come to the scene of the crime—Sam, who might know something he wasn't telling me. At least he was a place to start.

At home I got out of the uptown suit, patched up my face with some very needed makeup, and put on a skirt and a sweat shirt. Just as I was leaving the apartment, someone buzzed on the intercom. I jumped, thinking the street man had followed me home. I went to the window and peeked through the fire escape bars.

To my relief I saw a pair of tattered, yellowed Keds I recognized. The young reporter who'd tried to get information out of Sam at Lincoln Center was staring up at me, a lock of brown hair cutting across his forehead.

"Is it true you found the body? Can I talk to you?" He waved a steno notebook at me. "Brand new."

I smiled, thinking of Sam flicking this man's notes in the fountain. "Sure, come on up." When I heard him halfway up the four flights of stairs, I ran to the fire escape and climbed out and down.

Chapter Six

After a forty-five-minute ride, I ventured out of the "G" subway into Greenpoint, Brooklyn, "the garden spot of the univoise" according to a man I'd stopped for directions. I didn't see much greenery, but looking down Manhattan Avenue, I was treated to a startling view of the Citicorp Building across the river. In the haze, it looked like a giant lopped-off bar of silver.

Walking into calmer, cleaner back streets I found Sam's address, which turned out to be a *Polska Pierkania,* a Polish bakery. A bell rang when I opened the door, and a round, smiling woman, her hair as white and fluffy as meringue, hurried out from behind a flowered curtain with a tray covered with glistening mounds of nut-colored cakes. The smell of honey and jam gripped my stomach. In defense I breathed through my mouth and hurriedly asked if Sam Weston lived there. She beamed at the sound of his name.

"Tak, he is here, upstairs, in the back."

As I reached a dark-green wooden door in the back of the two-story house, the woman came hurrying after me, her slippers flopping against the cement walk.

"Ponczeks for Sammy," she said, giving me a plate with three puffy cakes. "You too." She unlocked the door for me and pointed a finger up the spotless wooden stairs to a pot of plastic red flowers sitting on the landing.

"It is good, a friend for Sammy," she said with a heavy accent of the home country. I nodded back, not at all sure he would consider me a friend.

I knocked at Sam's door, holding the plate in front of me as a peace offering. The door opened a crack, releasing a waft of beer and stale smoke. I saw a thin slice of face, then the door snapped shut, followed by a muffled "hold on a minute." His footsteps creaked away and back. A door closed. Whatever he was doing, it took him long enough for me to eat my *ponczek* and lick the plum jam it was stuffed with off my fingers. I was about to attack *ponczek* two, almost hoping he'd skipped out on me so I could eat all three, but the door opened.

"I wasn't dressed," Sam said. I looked down at his T-shirt grafted to his beer belly. That thing hadn't come off him in hours, if not days. I walked in, handing him the plate.

"You almost didn't get these," I said, wiping jam off my chin.

The room was long and narrow, furnished with two wooden folding chairs, a white, chipped kitchen table, a sagging chintz-covered convertible sofa, chintz curtains to match on the two windows, and pink hydrangea wallpaper. Sam caught my look. "She used to sew up here when her husband was alive. Now she has to run the bakery so I get to rent it, flowers included." He wiped his mouth with the back of his hand and lit a cigarette. "It's cheap."

92

An old, round-cornered refrigerator, the door repainted a yellower white than the original, stood against the far wall. On an antique rummage sale bureau sat an electric burner and a clean Pyrex coffeepot. A sad place. It felt transitory, without the imprint a man should leave in his home.

"What's up?" Sam put the *ponczek* plate on top of the turned-on TV. A Hawaii Five-O police car was chasing some bad guys, the volume down to a tiny wail. I recognized the habit that came from living alone too long.

I sat on the sofa. "I saw you at the Majestic this morning."

"Yeah?" He loomed in front of me with his football weight, in jeans and a red T-shirt that had been washed down to a dull pink. He looked odd without his baseball cap, younger.

"I was wondering what you were doing there?"

"How about you?"

"I found her."

"I don't wanna hear about it." Sam blew smoke toward the open window.

"Toni's being held for Johanna's murder, and I know he didn't do it."

"What do you want from me?"

I remembered what he'd said at my party. "Who would want to harm a beautiful thing like that." Had he seen something odd?

"That exposed cable Sunday night, was it really an accident, Sam? Couldn't it have been a first attempt to kill her?"

He walked to the refrigerator and took out two beers. "Even so, how's that let off Toni?" He offered me a can. I shook my head.

"There were a lot of people there," I said. "Two hundred extras that we know nothing about. Some crazed fan could have been among them. We've seen enough of that around. Maybe you noticed something about that nicked cable that you're not even aware of. Oh, please, Sam, think hard."

Sam's face relaxed. It could have been the long sip of beer or even the look of desperation that must have been on my face. He pulled over a chair and sat next to the TV. "It's a dumb way to kill anyone. Any one of those extras coulda touched the water and fried. Abe's alive only 'cause of his rubber-soled boots and a trained reaction to electrical danger. In our job, we've got to be quick, or we end up sunny-side up."

And in your job you know how to find out what's grounded and what isn't, I thought, remembering that the three hundred amps had traveled to the fountain because the sewer pipes weren't grounded.

Sam was giving me a slow, steady look from behind his beer can, maybe to check if he'd convinced me.

"When someone hates enough to kill," I said, focusing my eyes on his thick neck, "rules of logic spin out into space."

Sam took another long sip of beer.

"Why was Johanna scared of you?"

"Beats me." Did I notice a flicker? "Some actresses get real nervous. Seems to me that Italian gal's not easy to work for."

I remembered Sam trying to intimidate Sara that night at Lincoln Center, defending "Jo," and Johanna looking up in surprise. No one had called her "Jo" except Sam, and the *Post* that had spread JO

JUICED across the next day's paper.

The windows of Sam's room were open, and an occasional wind from the East River spread chintz flowers toward us. It was hot in the apartment anyway. The heat of the ovens below came through the soles of my shoes. So did the sweet smell of baking dough, through my soles, my bones, right up to my nostrils.

I inhaled deeply to give me a boost. "Have you worked with Johanna before?"

"No, far as I know this is her first New York film."

"How about Hollywood?"

"Naw, I'm strictly a Big Apple man."

His blue-and-yellow cap sat next to the uneaten cakes. On TV the car chase was over, and Ricardo Montalban, with a smirk on his face, was offering to make my biggest wish come true.

"You root for the L.A. Rams," I said, wishing Toni free from the New York police.

"Good team" was all I got for an answer. Two words and a blank face. I realized my amateur sleuthing wasn't getting me anywhere. Wood creaked outside the door, followed by a discreet knock.

"Sammy, perhaps your friend would like to stay for dinner? Tell her to stay for dinner."

"No, thanks, Mrs. Gorski," Sam called out.

"If you change your mind, I have plenty, you know I have always plenty for a friend. We all need friends, Sammy." He didn't answer, and after a few moments, we heard her creak down the stairs. I wondered if she'd been only thinking of Sam when she mentioned the need for friends.

"She's sweet, and she's a great baker. Does she

95

cook for you?"

Sam stood up and turned the TV off. That's when I noticed a series of small tears on the pink hydrangea wallpaper behind his head.

Sam followed my eyes. "Listen, I've gotta go," he said, shifting his weight.

Short gashes the width of Scotch tape. So white they looked newly torn.

"Sure, sorry," I said, standing up quickly and trying to keep my eyes from sweeping the contents of the apartment, wondering what had once been on that wall. I couldn't see Mrs. Gorski desecrating her flowered wallpaper. It had to be Sam. Was that why he had snapped the door shut in my face? Because there was something he had to get rid of?

"Can I use your bathroom? I'll only be a minute." I laughed, pretending embarrassment.

Sam hesitated a second, then pointed to a door catercorner to the entrance. I hurried over, locked the door behind me, and turned on the tap like any shy female about to pee. I had acted on a hunch, remembering the sound of a door closing while I waited outside on the landing. This was the only other door in the one-room apartment. Sam must have come here before letting me in.

The bathroom was square, roughly five by five feet, covered with shoulder-high peach-colored plastic tile topped by wallpaper painted over in white, the busy pattern of small flowers still showing through the single coat of paint. A white wicker shelf held the usual male toiletries and a dirty ashtray. A round hand-held mirror was nailed upside down above the sink, too high for me to see myself. There were no closed cabinets, nowhere really to hide anything. I looked in the shower, behind the toilet bowl, the water tank. Nothing except for a dead bee. The window was open, facing the one tree of the street and a neat row of houses that differed only in the patterns chosen for their plastic siding. Nothing that I could see had been thrown down on the spotless sidewalk. I lowered the toilet seat and sat on the edge. Maybe he had used the bathroom to pee; nothing more mysterious than that.

Sam opened the door to the corridor, banging it against the bathroom wall. He was anxious for me to go. I turned off the tap, flushed the toilet to keep up the pretense, and reached for the doorknob. My foot brushed the blue plastic shower curtain pushed to one side of the shower. A piece of tape, still brandishing a strip of pink hydrangea, popped out. I lifted one end of the curtain. A roll of torn magazine pages rested inside a fold. The top one, a thick, glossy sheet from *Vogue,* was upside down. Johanna smiled underneath a burst of Lacroix ruffles whose bright colors had faded. Her legs, sheathed in silvery stockings, waved up at me. I thought of pressed flowers.

Opening the door, I avoided Sam's face. "I'm sorry I took so long." Sam shifted his weight again, making the floor creak.

"I'm gone, gone. Thanks again." I rushed out of there, forgetting to take a last deep breath of glorious *Polska* bakery air.

Sam, a crazed fan, so obsessed with Johanna that he wanted her dead? I thought that over while I made my way back to Manhattan on the subway.

97

Johanna had accused him of stalking her. Was she telling the truth? Maybe. At least it was a possibility that might help Toni. Sam had been at the scene of the crime. Sam was a gaffer, and gaffers knew all about grounding. Gaffers used copper wire. I glossed over the fact that electrical knowledge was not exclusive to Sam, and that his tools were kept in the back of the generator truck where anyone could have snitched the wire. At that moment, unwanted details were like finding worms in my salad: they ruined my appetite.

"I have to talk to Toni's lawyer," I said as I walked into the darkened HearView screening room for the production meeting. I could barely make out Sara's, Diego's, and the DP's heads in the front row. The script girl, sitting in front of a small, dimly lighted desk against the soundproofed wall, looked up from her script and silenced me with a finger on her lips. On the screen Sara had got the shot she'd wanted.

SCENE 8.   EXT.   DAY.

CAROLE, the *City* reporter, comes out of the barbed-wired parking lot in Spanish Harlem with a determined, fast walk and hurries across the street toward protective trees just as the New Haven line train speeds across the stone bridge behind her.

The screen went blank, and for a few minutes, we sat in the dark in silence.

"The train of death," Sara said as the fluorescent lights switched on. She turned around and looked at me through her sunglasses, a yellow V on each side

98

of her nose for Varni and Victory. She looked bleached and wrinkled, as if she'd kept her face in the water too long. "How are you?" she asked.

I bent down and gave her a hug. Her shoulders trembled. "I want to talk to Toni's lawyer." I wanted to tell him about Johanna's reaction to Sam at my party, about his pictures of her. It was pretty flimsy stuff, but it might lead to more.

Diego, who'd stood up as I walked over, glanced at his steel Rolex. "He is with Toni at this very moment, I believe. He's due to telephone shortly."

"He's the best in New York," Sara said. "I insisted on the best. I don't care what it costs. No one in my troupe is a murderer." Her voice rose in pitch and the words speeded up. "It was some crazed, drugged-out American looking for publicity. John Lennon, Reagan, they shoot famous people for publicity. *Publicity!* Do you understand what this country has come to!"

It was useless to say anything. Diego tried to pat her shoulder, but she moved away.

Sara turned to face the blank screen and snapped her fingers at the script girl. "Lincoln Center. I want to see that again. Lincoln Center, please."

"You looked at that scene yesterday afternoon for more than an hour," Diego protested. "Why do you wish to see her again? Why worsen the situation?"

"Simona hasn't seen herself on film," Sara snapped back. "I want Simona to see herself on film."

Diego threw up his hands and sat down again. The lights went off, and a leader popped numbers at us on the screen. Ten, nine, eight . . . a beep on two.

If Sam had killed Johanna, why didn't he let her

99

die that first night?

The screen colored with people.

SCENE 4A.
EXT. LINCOLN CENTER. NIGHT.

PRIME MINISTER watches as CAROLE steps out of the fountain, dripping white jersey dress molded to her body.

Was it because the script called for Massimo to help her out, which would have meant he would have been jolted with three hundred amps too. Had Sam electrified the fountain in order to rescue her, maybe hoping for eternal gratitude by way of a tumble in bed? When that didn't work out, did he leash her with a piece of wire he had in his pocket? Possible.

Massimo slipped in the seat beside me, squeezing my hand. *"Poveretta,"* he said barely audibly. Poor thing. He looked up at the screen. In close-up, Johanna was delivering the line not written in the script.

CAROLE
This Venus isn't offering anything.
(She ignores PRIME MINISTER's extended arm.)
She can manage by herself.

CAROLE hikes up her dress to reveal her long legs and gracefully steps out of the fountain unaided.

A convenient line change for Massimo. He wouldn't have to touch her and she'd fry by herself.

100

Had he nicked the cable and pushed it against the drain valve? In a crowd of two hundred extras, that should have been easy enough to do without being noticed. He only had to stoop down, pretending to have dropped something, and then give the cable a good kick. The only problem was the sewer pipe. How would he have found out it wasn't grounded, that the electricity would run to the fountain? Maybe from one of Sam's electricians. They were always testing, looking for places to ground the lights. Massimo had been pretty upset with Johanna at my party, shaking her until her head rattled. Had he known about Toni all along? And what was Johanna going to reveal to *People?* What if Johanna wanted to leave him, for Toni or because she was bored? The junk media would have lighted the fireworks on that story.

MASSIMO MARINI DUMPED! FIRST TIME IN LATIN LOVER'S CAREER. HAS STAR LOST HIS SHINE?

For a vain actor who'd hit the half-century mark, it could have been a good enough reason to kill.

The lights came back on. Massimo looked at me from underneath eyelids at half-mast, a sad, gentle look that instantly made me feel guilty. I shook myself, wondering if I wasn't weaving suspects out of cobwebs in my brain. Maybe not. I made a mental note to call *People* in the morning.

Sara wiped her eyes. "You looked good on screen, Simona." I hadn't seen myself, and I suspected by the redness of her eyes, she hadn't either, but it got us over an awkward moment.

"What do we do now?" the DP asked. "Chuck everything?"

The phone rang. It was for Diego.

"If that's the lawyer, tell him I need to talk to him."

"What about?" Sara asked me.

"I just want to know how bad the situation is," I said. I wasn't about to advertise my suspicions.

Diego was at the desk, listening with hunched shoulders. The tension came clear across the room.

Diego hung up. "The lawyer's secretary has informed me that Toni's been arraigned for first degree murder. 'In record time,' according to her." He gave a sardonic smile. "Fortunately, he has been released on his own recognizance in deference to the consul general's personal guarantee." He spoke in the solemn tone of a funeral parlor director. "The consul is a good friend of my family's." He looked at Sara with a smug look on his face. "Of course, Toni has relinquished his passport voluntarily."

We discussed where Toni should go. I wanted him back with me, but Sara vetoed it. The media would hound him, he needed to be hidden. I reluctantly agreed even though I wanted him under my roof where I could fuss over him.

"How about the Gramercy Park Hotel?"

"No, no, his photo has made the *New York Times,*" Sara said, springing up from her seat. "Hotels are too public, all you need is a greedy concierge and the media appears."

"You can't recognize him from that picture," I protested. "His arm is over his face. So far, he's been able to keep his face hidden."

"Not for much longer unless he hides." She took off her sunglasses, and a triumphant gleam appeared in her eyes as she took a business card out of the breast pocket of her fuchsia shirt.

"What about this? Bed and Breakfast with a SoHo artist," she read. "Sounds wonderfully lewd, doesn't it, Diego? Don't you all think so?"

"Sara," Diego said simply, looking embarrassed.

"No one would think of looking for him there."

"*Brava,*" Massimo said. "Maybe I should go there too. I have been pursued by twenty reporters so far."

Sara laughed brashly. "You love it."

Diego was strongly against the idea. He thought a big hotel, the Sheraton for instance, was a better place. "Anonymity in the multitude," he said, sounding more pompous than usual.

"No, no," Sara said. "Toni goes to SoHo." Her tone made it clear she wasn't to be argued with. She gave Diego the number and pocketed the card. "Don't use his name, make up something. Outside, call outside. I don't want to hear you call in here."

As soon as Diego walked out the door, she sat cross-legged on the floor in front of the screen. She looked at Massimo, who hadn't budged from his seat the whole time, then at the DP.

"I don't think I can go on. The film was wrong from the start. It's not a Sara Varni film. It's Hollywood. It's crap. Crap, crap, crap, the whole thing is crap!"

"I don't do crap," Massimo said in a quiet voice.

"You'll do anything that will keep you on the screen," Sara snapped back. "Anyway, what's the point with no female lead?" There was an uncomfortable silence. It was the first time I'd seen Sara declare herself beaten.

"I saw a woman today who could finish the role," I offered, thinking of Hot Pink, who'd gone off to the movies with Greenhouse. "She looks enough like

103

Johanna to double her in long shots, maybe even a profile medium shot. Johanna only had the airport scene left, so it might work out."

Diego interrupted, saying there was room at the B and B and he'd left the address with the lawyer's secretary to give to Toni.

I reached for my bag. "I'm going there to wait for him. What name is he registered under?"

"No!" Diego said, holding up his hand. "For Toni's sake. You would lead the media straight to him. They are apparently waiting outside for any one of us to supply them with information."

I sat down again, playing along. I get very possessive about my friends when they're not doing well. Sometimes I think it might have to do with how well I'm doing. Maybe the worse off I am, the more possessive I get. Whatever it was, no one was going to keep me from Toni.

"Simona has a solution to our problem," the DP told Diego. I repeated about Hot Pink. "A friend of mine knows how to get hold of her. She really looks like her. Not as beautiful, but same build, hair, general coloring."

Diego started jingling his coins, his way of showing excitement. "Simona, find this young lady and bring her to the hotel tomorrow morning if possible. In the meantime, we can shoot various odds and ends with Massimo and the American agent. Central Park, for instance."

"I will not make money off a corpse," Sara said calmly. She was still sitting on the floor, her legs, in black tights, now stretched out in front of her. Her quadriceps twitched. "This whole project is repugnant."

"Sara's right," Massimo said. "Let's just go back home."

"Easy for you to say," Diego answered, his voice barely under control, coins jingling ferociously in his pocket. "You will move on to another film while the Varnis' film careers will be ruined." He walked over to Sara and leaned down. "There is too much money at stake, Sara," he said in a lowered voice. "The insurance is not enough to pay back the investors, and we are very much in debt, my love. This is the one commercial film that will finance your political films. We had an agreement, Sara, please don't forget." He spoke smoothly with no emotional inflection. "Please, Sara." That "please" sounded as if he were asking her for another cup of tea.

He started rubbing her shoulders, and Sara jumped up.

"I never wanted that woman," she yelled, waving her arms at the blank screen. "With all her beauty, she had no soul. She was as empty as the Coca-Cola cans your homeless rummage for in trash cans." She was looking straight at me. I was now the guilty American capitalist in her eyes, someone she could yell at comfortably. "As an actress, that's where she belonged. In the trash!"

"Sara, please," Massimo protested, standing up.

Sara stopped, her stretched-out arms frozen in front of her. Then her face collapsed into a mass of wrinkles, and she ran to Massimo to hug him. "Forgive me, forgive me, Massimino." She held his head against her shoulder as if he were a baby. "Yes, we'll finish the film. For you, Massimino, for you." She looked suddenly haggard, an old, defeated woman.

Her melodramatic excesses are taking their toll, I

thought coldly, wondering if she could have killed Johanna. She certainly had the temperament for it. Once she had slapped a bad actress hard, just to get the right mortified look for the shot.

Diego took her out of Massimo's arms. The two men looked at each other for a moment, obviously not liking what they saw.

"We will complete the film," Diego said, wrapping Sara with his arms. "But not for Massimo, for us." He gave a hint of a smile. "The situation for Massimo is not that tragic. Losing a woman to death might, after all, be easier than losing her to another man." Without letting the words take their toll on any of us, he went on, this time looking at me. "Find that woman and let me know." I bowed to his order and reached for my bag. He could have killed Johanna too, I thought, but he'd have waited until the end of the film, to make sure he'd got his five millions' worth.

Massimo followed me out. The manager of Hear-View unlocked the fire stairs for us so we could go out a back way and avoid the reporters. At the end of five flights, we walked into a vast windowless room stacked with rusting cans of 35mm film. After squeezing through a doorway piled high with garbage bags spewing magnetic tape, we stepped directly onto Broadway at the corner of Forty-ninth. Massimo slipped on his sunglasses even though the sun had shifted behind the western buildings. He walked quickly toward Times Square, hands stuffed in his pockets. No one looked at him long enough to recognize him. The crowd was too busy checking out souvenir T-shirts and Going Out of Business electronics. In front of us, a Japanese man pointed his video camera at the Circus Cinema marquee, which offered a triple feature: *Hot Fantasies, Daddy's Girl,* and *Debbie's Ecstasy.*

We walked past empty buildings plastered with film posters, underneath enormous blinking ads. Kirin Beer offered a twelve-foot glass of sparkling yellow. A giant camel's head, wearing sunglasses, promised us a cigarette with Smooth Character. I clutched my purse and wondered how many pockets were being picked by swift-handed locals. Massimo slowed down when I slipped my arm into his.

"Why were you fighting with Johanna in the bathroom?" I asked in a light tone, trying to pretend silly female curiosity.

He didn't buy it. "That's none of your business."

"Toni's a good friend."

"That doesn't make him innocent. He was in love with her, any idiot could see that."

"So were you. Does that make you guilty?"

Massimo looked up at the red and blue dots changing patterns like a giant kaleidoscope on the spectagram of the old *Times* Tower.

"I never understood Johanna. That's why I was in love with her, I think. One moment she'd be radiant, the next angry at the world."

Above the spectagram, the day's neon headlines appeared one letter at a time, wrapping themselves around the building. JEZEBEL DEVASTATES GULF. SEVENTEEN DEAD.

Somehow it seemed an appropriate headline.

"I wanted to keep her radiant." Massimo stopped at the corner of Forty-fourth and looked at the orange skyline. "A December wedding in Venice was her idea. It was the only way a man and a woman

107

should marry, she said. 'In the cold and the fog.' "
Massimo spoke slowly, a pained expression on his
face, as if words were something he disliked.

Ahead of us, in front of a boarded doorway, a
teenager with the sides of his head glistening stiffly
started yelling.

"Fuck, man, shit like you should be blown off the
streets with a bazooka!" He kicked a large packing
box at his feet, barely missing the man sitting next to
it, then did a cowboy amble toward his laughing
companions half a block up. That's the only time I'd
like to be a man. When I want to kick somebody's
balls up his throat in an even fight.

Massimo got to the ragged man before I did, making sure he was all right, stooping down to straighten
his box.

"Much obliged," the man said, tipping a non-
existent hat. "Handsome shoes you got there."

"You want them?" Massimo lifted a leg and un-
buckled one shoe.

"No, no, I don't take charity. My business is
noticin'." He got on all fours and crawled into his
box backward. "I observe, that's what I do."

Massimo extended a folded fifty-dollar bill. The
man's hand reached out of the box and swiped it
with the swiftness of a cat's paw.

"As I said, handsome shoes."

Massimo linked his arm in mine and began walking again.

"She was sad and I made her smile. You can't
imagine how strong that made me feel."

"Why was Johanna sad?"

Massimo shook his head. "Let's leave that with
her." He kissed both my cheeks and walked east on

Forty-fourth Street, the top flap of one shoe swinging loose. He'd forgotten to buckle it.

As I watched him walk toward the Royalton, I thought that Massimo was handsome, charming, even generous. He was also lazy and vain. What I didn't know was whether he was capable of murder.

Chapter Seven

Greenhouse was waiting on the steps of my apartment building, gulping a pistachio, chocolate-chip ice cream, his favorite. To my relief there was no sign of the reporter in Keds.

"You're a surprise," I said, unlocking the front door. I tried to look nonchalant, even though seeing him suddenly always shook me up as if I'd received an unexpected, extravagant gift. I never had him with me long enough to get used to his presence and stop marveling at the warmth of his face, the twinkle of his eyes, the incredibly touchable body.

"I thought you might need some cheering up," Greenhouse said, lifting the hair off my shoulders. I moved away from the kiss he was going to plant on the nape of my neck.

"Sex isn't going to do it," I answered and practically ran upstairs.

Greenhouse followed, closed the apartment door behind him, and watched as I kept busy straightening up the place.

"What are you scared of?" Greenhouse asked, gulping the last spoonful of ice cream. "I wasn't going to bang you on the front steps."

"Why not?" I dropped a week's stack of newspapers back on the floor: "That's all you ever seem to want."

"Not anymore than you do. Come on, Simona, be fair. I just came over to help, not to make love. But if ending up in bed makes both of us feel better, there's nothing wrong with that." He dumped the empty ice cream cup in the trash and sat down on the sofa beneath my loft bed. He looked so good that my heart did a quick tarantella. I walked away to sit on the windowsill, just to play it safe.

"I want more than good sex from you." In the year I'd been dating him I had never been this explicit. Fear of scaring him off—maybe even fear of getting more than I thought I deserved—had kept my mouth shut. Sometimes nursing an achy need can give a woman a perverse satisfaction. I used the ache to explain away all other failures.

"I'm a friend, I'm here, I want to help." Greenhouse leaned his elbows on his thighs and craned his neck toward me. "Look, you're very emotionally dependent, and I'm uncomfortable with that. My ex Irene was like that. For a long time, I thought that was just fine, and I swelled up my chest with pride taking care of her, Willy, myself, my friends. Well, it didn't work out. Irene got restless, upped and left, taking Willy with her. Now she depends on him so much I have to spend all my free time trying to get him to stand on his own."

"To stand on his own or to depend on Daddy?" I didn't like being compared to his ex.

Greenhouse leaned back against the pillows. "God, I hope I'm a good enough father not to do that to him."

111

"I may be emotionally dependent, but it hasn't been easy for me to find my feet in New York. In Rome I had a good career, a network of friends . . ." I laughed at that point, thinking of my best friend having an affair with my husband for five years, almost the length of my marriage, while dim-witted Simona suspected nothing until she caught them literally in her bed.

"I'm trying to start all over, I'm bound to limp a little." I left the windowsill and sat down in the armchair in front of him. "Give me a chance, I haven't asked to move in with you. I just want to talk to you more, see you more, know you better."

"You need too much love."

"You don't seem to mind in bed."

"No, I don't. That's when I want you as much as you want me. I guess what I'm trying to say is that I want to love a woman who's happy with herself, not happy just because a man loves her." Greenhouse's face turned red. It was the first time he'd mentioned the L word.

I leaned and kissed him lightly. He was right on about my waiting for a man to make me happy. I tried to find some excuses for being so old-fashioned. An Italian upbringing was a good one. Then I tried a domineering father who liked to yell a lot, then would rush me and my mother off to the movies to make up. It was partly true, but I also knew I was feeling sorry for myself after my divorce and was much more comfortable playing victim. I'd been strong enough to come to America to start over again, but that was all I'd been prepared to do. Since I had been so wronged, the rest was up to someone else, I'd thought.

After almost three years, America and her "you can do it" philosophy was slowly layering me with strength, giving me confidence. I had to start doing some of the work myself. "You're right, Greenhouse, I'll work on that," I finally said.

Greenhouse stood up and picked me off the chair. "You pull me in, Simona," he mumbled into my neck. "That's a little scary."

I liked the sound of that. "I'd love to meet Willy," I said, pressing my luck.

"How can I tell him there's a woman in my life when I'm trying to teach him to stand on his own? He'd take it as a betrayal."

"He's going to grow up a misogynist. Besides, there's nothing wrong with depending on people as long as we get the balance right. Isn't that what you were trying to tell me? Come on, Greenhouse," I shook him, enjoying the feel of his shoulders under my palms, "Talk to me about Willy, about what you do with your life the way you used to. In the past two months you've shut me out completely."

Greenhouse stiffened under my hands. "In the past two months, Irene has been badgering me to get back together for Willy's sake." I stepped back, dropping my hands.

"I love Willy more than anything in the world."

"What does that mean?"

"Whatever free time I've got I want to give it to Willy."

"A father's love is not what I'm trying to compete with."

"I know that."

"What about Irene? Is she in, out, what? I have a right to know that at least."

"Out. Out. She's out." He said it with vehemence. Too much for my liking.

"You're staying out of this case, right?" Greenhouse asked, sitting down again, in the far corner of the sofa this time. For once, we were both glad to change the subject.

"About the only thing Toni would kill is a roach." I was watching one walk across the kitchen sink at that very moment. I rolled up a newspaper and swatted it into a sticky brown mess. That was the mood I'd gotten into. "You ask me to be independent, yet you keep trying to control what I do."

"You almost got killed the last time you stuck your nose in a murder. I don't want you dead." Words of truce.

I went over to the fridge and took out a Fontana Candida bottle left over from the party. I poured two full glasses and offered him one. "Tell me what you found out. How did the murderer get into Johanna's apartment with an entire staff of doormen and janitors guarding the Majestic?"

"The service entrance doorman, an Indian, let in a man he thought was a waterproofer. You know they're doing all that work on the building." I nodded and gulped wine, spilling half of it down my white shirt.

"The man wore a hard hat, a big yellow slicker, boots. Anyway, the guy said he had to check on a scaffold rope that was caught in a tree on the nineteenth-floor terrace. The doorman buzzed Johanna, and she said it was OK for him to come up. Which

114

means she was alive at 6:05. The doorman remembers the time because he gets off at six and his replacement was late." Greenhouse sipped. His glass was just as full as mine, but his blue polo stayed dry. "The waterproofing crew denies there was a problem with the ropes. They stopped work as usual at four o'clock and everyone went home. They say no one went to the nineteenth floor at any time that day. The assistant D.A. thinks it was Toni."

"Didn't the doorman see the man's face?"

"He doesn't remember. He was worried about getting home in time for his son's birthday party." Greenhouse smiled at that point, I guess sympathizing with another father's dilemma.

"Then it could have been anyone."

"When Toni was kicked out of the Majestic earlier, he did say that nothing was going to stop him from seeing her. And Johanna did have his hair under her nails."

"Come on, Greenhouse, he'd spent the night with her. She could have grabbed his hair making love."

"I don't think so. Don't forget there was blood under her nails too. And Toni's got scratches on his scalp."

"Some people do funny things to get aroused."

Greenhouse put his glass down carefully and looked uncomfortable. "She was strangled from behind. The wire was twisted at the back of her neck. She probably reached behind her, pulling and scratching whatever she could get hold of. The overturned chair shows there was a struggle."

I finished the wine, thinking how short Toni is and how easy it would have been for Johanna to reach his head.

"You think he's guilty," I said angrily.

"The D.A.'s office thinks it has a good case." Greenhouse's face was glum. Suddenly I felt like a kid screaming in an empty house.

"I want to know what *you* think!" I slammed the glass down on my trunk. He gave me a pitying look that turned fright into fury.

"He's innocent," I yelled.

"Simona, when it comes to friends and lovers, you don't think with your head."

"What about you? You think you're so logical, good, and pure. You come to me in the middle of the night, without even a phone call just because your penis itches—"

"That's not true—"

"You come here to tell me to stay out of the case, with about as much sensitivity as a rattlesnake you tell me Irene wants you back, you tell me one of my best friends is a murderer—and you want me to think with my head? My head's a fried mess! How the hell do you expect me to use my brain!"

"Jesus, I hate this."

So did I, but I couldn't help myself. I couldn't even begin to deal with the thought of Irene coming back into his life. I scrounged around the pile of trash I'd collected earlier and found the blue pack of Gauloises Massimo had left the night of the party. I took out a crushed cigarette, carefully straightened it, and lighted it. I inhaled, at that moment enjoying the awful taste of that pitch-black tobacco. Greenhouse hated me to smoke. I sat back in my chair. "Who's the Hot Pink blonde you went to the movies with last night?"

Greenhouse looked surprised. "We just work out at the same gym." He reached over and touched my hand. "Why didn't you let me know you were there? There's no reason to be jealous."

Being on a satisfyingly destructive bent, I wasn't about to make peace. "I'm sorry to delude you, Detective Greenhouse, my curiosity is purely professional. Hot Pink looks enough like Johanna Gayle to double for her in long shots and fast action shots. As you recall, we've just lost the star of our movie. Diego and Sara want to meet her."

Greenhouse went over to the sink and washed his glass. "Linda Shaw. She lives in Chelsea, Twenty-first and Eighth."

"You wouldn't happen to have her phone number?" I asked sarcastically.

"She's in the phone book." He left without saying another word.

I finished the bottle and the cigarettes while it got dark outside. For once, I was fully aware I'd completely fucked up.

Around ten o'clock I called Greenhouse's apartment and apologized to his answering machine for taking out my whole life on him. It was cowardly to apologize to a tape, but I had no idea when he was coming home, and I wanted him to know how sorry I was as soon as possible. I was even rash enough to promise I would use my head from now on. To myself more than to him.

I looked up Linda Shaw's number in the phone

book and dialed. By the sound of her voice, Linda thought life was just a reggae shake. She had never heard of Sara Varni, but she gurgled that she'd love to meet Massimo Marini, he was so handsome, and did I know she was a gym teacher and could do all sorts of stunts if that those were needed, like triple somersaults and splits.

I found her wearisome, but then I was jealous, not only of her possible relationship with Greenhouse but of her enthusiasm. I gave her Diego's phone number at the Royalton to set up an appointment right away. Then I called Raf, Greenhouse's partner, at home. I asked him to find out what he could about Sam Weston.

"Ehi, I can't. Lover boy is my partner, *mi amigo.* He told me you were staying out of this one."

"I'm afraid for Toni. I can't help him all by myself. Please, Raf."

"I don't know. I gotta clear it with Stan first."

"Oh, God, he'll never say yes!"

There was a pause, then Raf said, "I'll see what I can do." I practically burst into tears of relief.

"You've been good to me. By the way, Mama is going to stay another month, ain't that right, *Mamacita?"* Raf called out. I heard an enthusiastic *"Si, si"* in the background. "Another month. Isn't that great?" I laughed.

"The place is yours whenever you want." I'd been loaning my apartment to Raf and his girlfriend Tina ever since his mother had come from San Juan for a "short" visit, now entering its third month. Tina lived with her parents and four younger brothers, which made privacy impossible. Twice a week

118

I'd work late, go to the movies, or wait up at Tania's. After they left, I always found a made-over bed, a clean kitchen, and great leftovers cooked by Raf, "the best paella maker in the five boroughs," as he liked to call himself.

"Thanks, Simonita. What is it you wanna know?"

I told Raf what I knew about Sam: name, address, telephone number, and union. I was hoping he'd furnish me with a lot more. My crazed-fan theory about Sam was too slim to present to Toni's lawyer, I'd decided. I was looking for a stronger connection between Sam and Johanna, and I had a hunch Sam had known Johanna off the set. It wasn't because he collected pictures of her, any fan would do that, crazed or not. It was Johanna's strong reaction to his presence at my party, and the weary, sad tone of his voice when he had told "Jo" she was out of her mind and needed help that had stayed in my mind. His words had sounded as if they'd been repeated many times.

Before hanging up, Raf added, *"Ehi,* tonight lover boy sounded like his *cojones* had dropped in the blender. You two have a fight?"

"Yeah, my fault."

"You both got asses for brains. You're made for each other. *Un beso.*"

"A kiss to you too. Love to Tina."

Feeling a bit better for having put something in motion, I packed Toni's overnight case, strapped his Leica around my neck, and making sure no Keds were following me, I walked over to the Bed and Breakfast place in SoHo.

The building was on Greene Street at the corner

of Prince, a rusty cast-iron building desperate for a paint job. I was buzzed up, and a thin blonde girl, around seven years old, opened the metal door of the third floor.

"My name is Tiffany. My mom's gone for cigarettes and candy." She looked behind me as if surprised I was alone. I noticed she was wearing a sopping wet apron. "Do you want to rent a room?"

I didn't know what name Diego had used for Toni so I just said I was a friend of the man who had reserved a room that day. Tiffany let me in with a big smile, telling me they hadn't had a guest in two weeks. She seemed happy to have company.

The place was a floor-through with a cast-iron, patterned ceiling painted the color of egg yolk and wide wooden floorboards splattered with paint. A curtain of plants held up by macramé baskets covered the two long windows at both ends. Tiffany led me along a Pompeian red plasterboard wall that had been added to create separate rooms behind a row of columns. She opened the last door and showed me where Toni was going to sleep, a simple room covered with Abstract Expressionist art in garish colors. They were all done by the same hand, probably the owner, I thought, wondering what kind of nightmares would lead an artist to paint those slashes. The single narrow window faced a wall. A large, tightly embroidered electric blue Chinese shawl almost covered the queen-size bed. A smaller shawl, a deep rose, was draped over a wobbly standup lamp, the only light in the room. I left Toni's case on the floor, thinking the place would have made a perfect bordello.

Tiffany had gone to the open kitchen, on the entrance side of the loft. She was standing on a low wooden stool in front of a double sink piled high with dishes. The round kitchen table to one side, set for three, hadn't been cleared since breakfast. One mug was still filled with coffee and a floating lipsticked cigarette butt. I vaguely wondered if Mom had a boyfriend. Tiffany had made no mention of Dad.

"Want some help?" I asked, picking up the dishes from the table and setting them on the wooden counter. Tiffany bobbed her head yes. I washed, she dried. It was nice to have this lithe pretty girl next to me, silently watching me with small, curious blue eyes set deep in her long face. I imagined Greenhouse and Willy spending a night together, sharing chores after the movies or a game, father and son close, shutting out the world for fear it might change their love for each other. I couldn't really blame him for keeping Willy to himself. If I had a child, I might have done the same thing.

"Are you a friend of Johanna's?" Tiffany asked while I was reaching up to put the last set of dishes into a blue cabinet. I nearly dropped the whole stack.

"Johanna? You know Johanna?"

Tiffany walked to a big wire-mesh trash can, the kind found on New York street corners. Next to it was a pile of newspapers higher than the one I had at home. She took out the fourth paper down and showed me the old *Post* with JO JUICED and Johanna's picture spread across the front page. Tiffany brushed the page with a small, wet hand, circling

Johanna's face with her index finger.

"She's real pretty," Tiffany said. "Don't you think she's pretty?"

"Very. Why do you think I knew her?"

"Did the man who's coming here kill her?"

"No!" I said too loudly. Tiffany winced. I crouched down next to her. "You mustn't be afraid. He liked her. He liked her an awful lot, he wouldn't kill her." How did she know about Toni? Had Diego been so stupid as to register Toni under his own name? "You'll see, Toni's too nice to hurt anyone." Tiffany's eyes darted to the front door covered by purple and black X's.

"Don't be afraid," I said. She had stroked Johanna's photograph with awe in her face. Was she just another adoring fan, or did she know her?

"Afraid of what?" A busty woman in her late thirties with a bush of frizzy mango-colored hair examined me with her eyes without surprise. "You look harmless enough."

"That's my mom," Tiffany said, pointing to her with a finger. Mom didn't have Tiffany's delicate looks. She had a wide face with strong cheekbones and a squat nose that spread out at the nostrils as if she'd had the door slammed in her face. She walked toward us in a sloppy, to-hell-with-it way that made her sensual, even though she was not attractive.

Tiffany took the paper bag from her mother. "No snitching," her mother warned, throwing the keys in an empty giant popcorn can by the door. "Never lose them that way." She pulled back her hair with both hands and looked over the neat kitchen. "Great, the dishes are done. I hope you didn't

122

help Tiffany, she's got to learn to do them herself. Teaches her not to be lazy."

Tiffany had opened the bag, removing a bottle of amaretto and three packages of Malomars. She looked at her mother, her jaw set with disappointment.

"Thought I forgot, eh?" Mom whipped out a half-pound bag of M&M's from under a large, dirty turquoise shirt and tossed it to Tiffany, who instantly beamed and ran with it to her room.

"What do you need, a single, a double?" Mom bit into a Malomar and reached for a glass from the blue cabinet above the sink. The back of her jeans had slits just below her behind. A lot of dappled flesh showed through as she stretched up.

"The name's Bella." She wiggled fingers in greeting while she poured amaretto in a large wineglass. "Not really, but that's what my ex called me."

I explained I was here to see Toni Berto. She sat down at the round table, offering me the bottle, which I declined, and then dipped a Malomar in her glass. She'd slowed her movements at the mention of Toni's name, as if she were stalling for time.

She took a big bite of the chocolate-covered marshmallow. "Anthony Varni's the man I'm expecting tonight."

"That's him," I said with a short laugh, sitting down opposite her. "He's an actor. Varni's his stage name." Diego hadn't been very imaginative, and the problem with having used his own name was that Sara and he had both been mentioned in the papers in connection with Toni and the murder. Maybe that was how Bella had figured out who Toni really was, and then told her seven-year-old daughter so that Tiffany could have some colorful nightmares to add to the place. I wondered who else had been told. Hopefully not the press.

"My ex was an actor. Italian, too." Bella pronounced it Eyetalian. Her tongue flicked down on her chin to lick up a drool of almond liqueur. "One night he said he was going for a slice of pizza up at Arturo's on Houston, and that was that." She offered me a Marlboro, and I remembered about my promise to use my head. I reluctantly said no.

"She was quite a slice. Skin as milky as mozzarella and about seventeen years old. Too bad, I liked the guy." Bella smoked between dripping bites, never giving her mouth a rest. "Italians make the best damn lovers. It's in the hands, you know." She waved her hands. I noticed she was a nail biter. "Ten fingers workin' your body . . . hey, I don't need to tell you, you're Italian, right? The minute I saw you, I said I bet she's Italian. The nose gives you away. Long and straight like my ex. You've got an accent too. Not much, but I'm good at picking up accents. I said if she's Italian, she's going to want to eat a lot, breakfast comes with the room, and Tiffany only got one croissant from Dean and DeLuca, so it's a good thing you aren't staying. Why do you Mediterraneans eat so much? My ex gulped down food like a pig."

I didn't know where Bella was from, but she'd already finished one pack of Malomars by now and had poured herself another glass of amaretto. I said nothing, uncomfortable with her labels. It had started to rain hard. Rivulets of water scurried

124

down the dirty panes of the two long windows above the kitchen counter, reflecting the fluorescent light in moving bands, like glowworms. Where the hell was Toni?

"Did you know Johanna Gayle?" I asked.

Bella stubbed out her cigarette and stared back at me with big, wet brown eyes, giving me a slow, crooked smile with her full lips.

"Naw," she finally answered. "Though she was just like that pizza slice my husband left me for. Milky white. At least on screen."

Someone buzzed the intercom, and Bella walked barefoot to the door to ask who it was.

"Toni Varni."

Bella opened the purple and black door and leaned against it. She looked at the streams of rain pouring down the windows. "Pizza Slice's the one who should have gotten her throat squeezed."

Toni looked awful, like something dragged out of an oil spill. I tried to hug him, wet as he was, but he wouldn't let me. Bella handed him a towel from a tousled pile on top of the dryer and asked him to remove his sopping shoes. She dropped them on top of the tall stack of newspapers, quickly flipping the *Post* Tiffany had left on top so that Johanna's photo didn't show. She had figured out who Toni was all right.

Once Toni had dried off, he didn't look much better. He hadn't shaved, his round face sagged, and he looked at me with red-veined eyes that made me think of cracked glass. I decided to spend the night with him.

"A double'll be fifteen dollars more, eight-five

dollars in all," Bella said when I told her, throwing me a towel.

I reached for my credit card in my purse and offered it.

Bella shook her head. "I only take cash. And you'll have to share the croissant, unless you like Malomars."

Lying in Bella's double bed in the dark, Toni refused to talk, saying he hadn't slept in forty-eight hours. He fell asleep in his boxer shorts with his head on my shoulder while I stroked the back of his neck. After an hour, he screamed, clutching the neck of my sweat shirt. I shook him awake. Finally, around two o'clock in the morning, we began to talk. I held him, my caresses only gestures of affection.

"Why did Johanna have your hair and blood under her nails?" I twisted one of his red curls around my fingers. Toni hesitated.

"Strong sex?" I offered. He moved away and turned on the lamp draped with the small Chinese shawl. A dim pink glow filled the room. He looked at me, disappointed.

"I know you've had enough questions," I said, sitting up cross-legged on the bed. "But I want to help. If I can just find another strong suspect, you'll be OK. Come on, Toni, you always thought I could make things work. Help me. At least tell me what you told the police."

He was embarrassed, pulling at the blue silk fringe of the shawl that still covered the bed. "Johanna had strange tastes in bed. She liked me to treat her badly, hurt her. Then she liked to hurt back. It was the only way she got pleasure."

I remembered Johanna's feminist stance that first night at Lincoln Center, wanting to minimize the appeal of her body in favor of her brains. How had she reconciled that with her tastes in bed?

"Did you tell the police?"

"I just said we were very active. I don't want them to think she was perverse. They wouldn't believe me anyway. There were no signs on her body. She always made sure I left no telltale signs on her body."

"How'd you manage that?"

"She knew all the tricks." Toni pulled up the shawl and started folding it neatly into a small square. "Johanna had been abused as a child. An older cousin, she said. I think the abuse lasted a long time because of the way she made love. It had to be painful. She couldn't conceive of any other way of doing it. If I refused, I didn't love her." Toni shook the shawl open and started folding again. "She'd say giving and accepting pain was a way of showing love."

Johanna had always put me off by what I'd thought was a greedy intensity that somehow didn't fit in with the rest of her. Now I wondered if that "intensity" hadn't been a need for healthy affection, a need so gnawing it broke through what Toni called her "cashmere" skin. That need would make her betrayal of Toni and Massimo understandable, even forgivable.

"Do you think the abuser could be the killer?"

The pink light from the lamp gave Toni's tired face a soft, baby quality. "No, she said she got free of him a long time ago."

"Why did you call her 'a bitch in heat' in front of everyone?"

He told me he'd been crazy with jealousy. Johanna had lied about Massimo, denying they'd been lovers. After my party, Massimo had unexpectedly gone over to the Majestic, and Toni had listened from Johanna's dressing room while Massimo demanded to know what she was going to tell *People* the next day.

"Johanna just kept laughing and moving around the room as if she were dancing. I heard the swish of her silk nightgown and stooped down to look through the keyhole. Massimo was sitting on the bed, begging her to marry him as she'd promised. She just twirled around the room. He sounded like he was crying. She stopped laughing and, in her lowest, grating voice, told him to leave. She used that voice to pretend she was in command. She liked to use it making love, when it was my turn to play victim."

"What did you tell the police?"

"Nothing about the abuse." He grabbed my shoulders. "You can't tell anyone about the abuse. That's not getting spread on some filthy front page." He let go of me and leaned against the iron bedstead, closing his eyes. "I did tell them about Massimo. Just that he had come to her apartment that night wanting to know about the magazine article. I didn't tell them the state he was in. I couldn't do that to him."

128

"Oh, Toni!" I leaned over and kissed him. "When are you going to learn to defend yourself!"

Toni flicked his finger lightly against my cheek. "You're going to do that for me, right?"

"Right."

I turned off the light and settled down, fully dressed, to sleep next to my sweet, honorable, well-meaning friend, wondering for the first time how the hell I was going to help him when he wasn't willing to help himself.

Chapter Eight

When I woke up the next morning, Toni had gone. A note told me he was taking pictures of Chinatown, then meeting the lawyer at the Criminal Courts building downtown to be indicted. Greenhouse had told me that getting arraigned and indicted in forty-eight hours was practically unheard of in the New York City justice system, which meant that the rookie assistant D.A. was very sure he had his man. It seemed as if his mind was closed to other possibilities. Or else he was simply stupid, more interested in making headlines than making justice. Either way, it didn't look very good for Toni.

After a quick shower, I looked for Bella to ask if I could use her phone, but the only open door led to Tiffany's empty room. All the better, I would have some privacy. I walked down to the kitchen area and noticed that the stack of newspapers had disappeared, but the amaretto bottle and the wineglass were still on the kitchen table along with the Malomar boxes. Everything was empty.

The phone was on a corner of the kitchen

counter, half hidden by a gallon of turpentine. The first call I made was to Greenhouse at the precinct.

"I got your message," Greenhouse told me, his voice not particularly friendly, for which I didn't blame him after the way I'd treated him.

I thumbed a notepad next to the phone and plunged ahead. "I promised you I'd use my head." I heard coughing behind the door directly to my left and dropped my voice to a whisper. Bella would be only too happy to listen in on my emotional problems, to add them to her list of Italian quirks.

"The fight we had was just stupid. I don't ever want to be like that again. From now on, I'm going to try standing on my own, being happy with myself, and all that self-help business, but that means no Greenhouse in my life for a while, since the sight of you makes my knees and brains wobble. Besides, you've got some thinking to do on your end too. So when I decide my leg and head muscles are working again and you decide Irene is definitely an ex, we might meet over a bowl of pasta." I stopped, relieved I'd got through my little speech in one hoarse breath. Discovering Johanna's desperate needs had scared me into giving my own life some serious thought during the night. I could in no way compare her horrifying trauma to my divorce pains, but here I was still basically feeling sorry for myself and wanting Greenhouse to save me. It was time to say *Basta!* Enough! If I didn't get rid of my limp soon, one day I might not get up at all.

All I was getting from the other end of the phone was silence. I felt as though I'd just talked to a wall.

"Well, Greenhouse, aren't you going to say anything? A 'Good for you' or even better 'I'll kill myself without you.' How about a mild response like 'Fuck off?' " My voice cracked on the last two words.

"Are you crying?"

"Hell, no, Greenhouse!" My voice was good and loud now. "I'm trying not to wake up the whole household." How *dare* he think I was crying! I was just having a horrible time listening to a silence that, to me, meant he didn't care.

"Who's with you?"

"I'm not home."

"Where the hell are you then?"

A frizzy mass of mango-colored hair peeked out of the nearest door to my left. Bella looked at me sleepily, a cigarette already in her mouth. I waved fingers at her.

"Never mind where I am. Did what I said sound reasonable? It does to me." More silence. "Dammit, Greenhouse! Talk to me!"

"Simona, where are you?" He was using his tough investigative-cop tone, the one that was supposed to make the killer confess all.

"I can't tell you, I'm sorry."

"Hell, then do what you want. You already have anyway." He banged the phone down.

I stood there, the receiver still attached to my ear, trying to hold on to the connection. He was angry, maybe even jealous. I didn't know. That was the hard part. I'd dated this man for a year, made love only to him, and I didn't know what he was feeling or thinking. As for my feelings, I was scared.

Bella had closed her door again. I dialed the operator for the telephone number of *People* magazine, jotted it down on the notepad I'd thumbed nervously into a neat row of paper curls, and dialed again. I asked for the editor of the Johanna Gayle story; a cheerful voice told me she would put me through to Mr. Farnsworth, Ms. Gerard's assistant.

I introduced myself to an unhurried voice from the South. He was very sorry that Ms. Gerard was out of town for the rest of the week, and what might he do for me?

"I worked with Johanna Gayle on the set of *Where Goes the Future?* I'm the one who found her dead, and I want to give Ms. Gerard the exclusive story."

He stopped breathing at that news. I had no intention of giving anyone anything on Johanna, but if I was to get any information out of Ms. Gerard, I had to offer some bait. I planned to repeat what the police had already released to the media, how I had found her, adding how I had been too shocked to remember much, how lovely she had been to work for, and if that wasn't enough I would invent a few emotional details along the way. The detail of my throwing up on Johanna's BLONDES HAVE MORE FUN needlepoint pillow was right down their gutter, but that was one of the many things I was going to keep to myself.

"I hear you," Mr. Farnsworth finally said. "But why Ms. Gerard? Wouldn't someone else do? She really is out of town on another story." He strung out his words, one heavy syllable after another, without pause, not giving me a chance to answer. "I'd consider it a privilege to work with you. I truly mean it. I have always been a great fan of Miss Gayle's." He sucked in his breath slowly, probably tasting his first big break in the gossip business.

I explained that Johanna Gayle had planned to be interviewed by Ms. Gerard the day of the murder, and therefore Ms. Gerard had probably prepared an extensive background file on her. She was the logical choice.

I wasn't really interested in biographical details; I just wanted to know why Massimo was so worried about that interview. If Ms. Gerard had had any preliminary talks with Johanna, she might be able to tell me.

"I hear you, you want to barter information." He wasn't dumb. "No need to feel queasy about it, it's done all the time. Where do you happen to live?" I told him.

"Fantastic, meet me at the southeast corner of Hudson and St. Luke's at one o'clock. There's a special little retreat called The Writer's Corner, owned by a friend of mine. Lunch is on the magazine. I'll bring the file, you bring you. You make my acquaintance, you like me, you talk. You don't like me, you enjoy the best cherry pie in town. May I consider that a deal?"

"You may," I said after a beat, momentarily distracted by what I'd just recognized in Bella's note-pad. Almost hidden by a maze of squiggles were the numbers 869-4400, 702. Next to it was a rough sketch of a man's square-jawed face.

"So you get to eat the whole croissant."

I turned around. Bella was standing behind me, wearing a graying T-shirt that clung to her large, pear-shaped breasts and barely covered her crotch. Her mauve-colored lips clamped the tail end of a Marlboro. She hadn't bothered combing her hair or putting on anything else.

"Your boyfriend left at dawn. I heard him tip-toeing out."

"Do you know Diego Varni?"

"You mean Anthony Varni?"

"No, I mean Diego Varni." I showed her the pad. "This is the Royalton Hotel number, and 702 is the number of his room. And this sketch looks exactly like him."

She took the pad from me and looked at the scribbled sheet without blinking, then walked over to the table and sat down.

"How do you know him, Bella?"

"You're a nosy bitch, aren't you? Just like my mother-in-law. She used to unbutton my blouse to see if I was wearing a clean bra. I stopped wearing them, that really freaked her out." Bella dropped her cigarette butt into the empty wineglass and covered it with a hand. "OK, I'll tell you. Yester-day, this man with an accent calls me to reserve a room, he doesn't know for how long." She kept her eyes on the glass, watching it fill up with smoke. "He gives me his name, Mr. Diego. I remember thinking Diego was a great name for an Italian, you know, Diego, Dago." Bella split her mauve lips open and grinned. "This Diego says he's going to give Toni the money to pay for the room, but if there are problems, I should ask for that room number at the hotel. So that's how I have his number." She released her hand from the glass; smoke swirled out and disappeared.

She'd made perfect sense, but I didn't want to believe her. "How did you know Toni was the man suspected of Johanna's murder? He hadn't even come here yet, and Tiffany knew all about him."

"Jeesus, what else do you want! Look, when I ask this Diego for Toni's last name, the man hesitates, then says I should register him as Anthony Varni. Now I got no TV in the place, it's bad for Tiffany and my creativity, but I do read the papers, especially the crime stuff, so I make the connection. Mr. Diego and Anthony Varni become Diego Varni. From there, it's easy to figure that the Anthony that's coming here is Anthony Berto, known as Toni." Bella tore the top sheet from the notepad and balled it up in her hand. "Want some coffee with your croissant?" She walked over to the stove in bare feet and turned on the gas burner under a chipped red enamel teakettle. "It's Medaglia D'Oro instant, real strong like you guys like it." She threw the balled-up sheet under the kettle and watched it burn.

"That doesn't explain the sketch you made of Diego. It's a good likeness, by the way. You should do more portraits."

Bella walked to the front door and opened it.

"People make me sick. I prefer to paint my own thoughts." She leaned across the threshold, giving me a full view of her bare rump, then straightened up and threw a newspaper at me. It was the same *Post* Tiffany had shown me. On the front cover was the picture I had shown Toni the morning after the fountain accident. Diego stood next to Johanna in front of a limousine. The expression on the sketched face matched the one in the photo perfectly.

Bella gave me that crooked mauve smile of hers again, and I felt like an idiot. "Mr. Diego looks like he knows what's up," she said. "That's the kind I go for. By the way, your friend skipped without paying. Do you have the money?"

I reached in my purse and pulled out eighty-five dollars. "Mr. Varni can pay the rest if Toni stays." I put the bills on the counter. "For breakfast, Toni only eats bacon and eggs with lots of hash-brown potatoes, and you can put that on Mr. Varni's bill too." I went through the purple door and took the stairs down two at a time.

The street was still wet from last night's rain. I turned right on Prince Street and got whipped in the back by a cold wind tunneling across from the Hudson River. I hugged myself and quickly walked east, past elegant stores and garbage bags piled on the curb like Bowery bums.

Tiffany stood at the far corner of Broadway, holding a carton of Marlboros under her arm and gawking at a geometric display of international chocolates in Dean & DeLuca's window. She looked like a waif.

I ran across the street shouting, "Come on, Tiffany, let's go for all the chocolate you can eat." She clapped her hands and ran ahead of me through the wide doors of the D&D food palace.

We were practically the only ones in the place; SoHo and the Village don't wake up before noon. I perched her on top of the marble stand-up counter near one window while I got two foamy cappuccinos with lots of cocoa on top and a chocolate-filled bun.

Tiffany fiddled with the cigarette carton, her legs swinging back and forth, apparently having second thoughts.

"Don't worry. Mom won't mind," I said, not caring whether Bella minded or not. I had the feeling Tiffany was in need of a good spoiling. I sipped, watching her split open the bun and lick the chocolate. "There's more where that came from." She smiled and bit into it.

"Are you Johanna's best friend?" she asked with a dark brown mouth.

"I'd just met her," I said, spreading her napkin neatly across her lap. Tiffany put her half-eaten bun down and reached inside her pink dress, pulling out a gold locket in the shape of a heart.

"Did she give you this?"

Tiffany nodded, her face tight now. "It's from Tiffany's. I have the blue box to prove it. I even kept the white ribbon." She tucked the locket back in her dress and patted it. "Really, she gave it to me."

"I believe you."

"Mom says people will say I'm lying."

"Where did you meet Johanna?"

"At home. She'd come to stay some nights. When she didn't like her house."

So Bella had lied after all. What had Johanna been doing there? Maybe running away after her father's death. It was hard to stay alone in a place that had once been shared. I remembered that from my divorce.

"Have you known her a long time?"

"I don't remember, but Mom said once it was four years." Before her father's death then.

"Did she come alone?"

"Yes."

A man dressed entirely in black with pageboy-length hair and small, blue-tinted round glasses came up to the counter followed by a younger man dressed exactly like him. To make room, I picked up Tiffany and stood her on the floor while the two men argued over the right shade of moiré silk needed for Mrs. Aschcroft's bathroom.

Tiffany wandered off to stare at a stuffed brown hen perched on top of a barrel of "Yukon gold" potatoes. I followed.

"Did Johanna always come alone?"

"You're ugly!" Tiffany swung at the hen, her face contorted with anger. I held her back with one arm and steadied the hen with the other.

"Why don't you hit me, Tiffany? Come on." I crouched down and raised both hands, palms facing her. "A big punch, like Mike Tyson." What else do you say to a kid who's trying to deal with death.

Tiffany shook her head. "She said I looked like

her when she was a little girl." Tears began to shine her cheeks. "That's what she told me, that I looked like her."

"You do. You're just as pretty." I hugged her and offered my paper napkin. "I'm sorry," I said, feeling awful that I'd provoked those tears. It was tough to care for a child, I thought, her feelings always looming larger than life, engulfing your own, her need the center of her being. Was that what Greenhouse was dealing with? Even reconsidering an ex-wife he no longer wanted to keep his son happy? There was no way I could know, the way I didn't know why Bella had lied, why Johanna had sought refuge in her loft, who had killed her.

Tiffany cleaned her face and shifted her glance to a table piled with chocolate bars. I let her pick six bars, stopping myself from asking more questions. I'd done enough damage to her and myself for the day. Did I really want to manage without Greenhouse? Was this independence so necessary?

We went back to the marble counter and our cappuccinos. I thought about Sara whipping out Bella's business card, insisting Toni hide there while the two decorators narrowed down Mrs. Aschcroft's shower curtain selection between copper green and bronze gold. Did Sara know that Johanna used to go to that B&B? If she did, sending Toni to hide there would certainly appeal to her director's love of dramatic coincidence. Somehow I doubted Johanna had told her about the place. The more likely explanation was that Johanna had left a card lying around, and Sara had found it.

By the time I had finished my thoughts and my cappuccino, copper green with gold braiding had won the day.

"My curtain is plastic," Tiffany volunteered to the decorators, "and my mom painted it with Mondrian squares."

We left the two horrified faces and walked back against the wind to Tiffany's rusted building. She let me kiss her good-bye, and I avoided the temptation to follow her back up to challenge Mom. I was pretty sure Tiffany would have borne the brunt of it the minute I left.

At one o'clock I was sitting in the Writer's Corner, a cozy room with differently shaped wooden tables against the walls and windows and an oak rolltop desk in the middle. A typewriter that looked as though it might have been dug up in Pompeii held the day's menu. The walls were lined with books and pictures interrupted by old photographs of illustrious writers. I recognized Hemingway and F. Scott Fitzgerald looking down at the lunch crowd with boozed-up eyes. In a drawing, Edgar Allan Poe, who had lived around the corner, held a raven on his uplifted palm. Mr. Farnsworth hadn't arrived yet, so I kept busy watching a softball game being played across St. Luke's Place, on a playground that had once been a cemetery. The wind had cleared the sky of rain clouds, and the fall sun brightened the ginkgo trees to a squeaky shine.

"Miss Griffo?" It sounded more like Miss Grievo. I recognized the southern accent and looked back. It was my day for surprises.

"But you're . . ."

"One and the same." He sat down and crossed his long legs. A time-yellow Ked stared up at me.

"There are no fire escapes here for a quick getaway," he said, catching my unhappy look. "Although there is a door. But do stay. I'm harmless."

He did look harmless, his tall body uncomfortably bent over the café chair, a shock of straight dark hair falling over his forehead. He was young, thirty at the most, and wore a tired tweed coat, a badly knotted bow tie over a blue button-down shirt that hadn't seen an iron since he left his momma, old khakis, and no socks. Quite harmless, I decided. Besides he had a file I wanted, now lying on the table in front of me.

"You should have told me who you were over the phone."

He cocked his head. "I did, I believe. I simply omitted the fact that I had already seen you at Lincoln Center and leaning out of your apartment window. But you're perfectly right, this is a bad beginning." He unfolded himself, towering over me. "Pretend you've never seen me, although I can't say I can do the same with you." He extended a knuckly hand. "Jonathan Farnsworth, fairly new at the reporting game and loving it. Charmed to meet you. And I do mean that."

I wasn't about to be taken in by his charm. Not on my first day of independence at least. I shook his hand. "Simona Griffo. May I look at the file?"

"Whoa! Where I come from, we do things in a more civilized way. Food and drink first." He called the waiter over by name and ordered a double portion of cherry pie and iced tea, while I asked for a smoked trout salad and plain water.

Over lunch I tried several times to bring the talk to Johanna, but he'd have none of it. He told me about his home in Williamsburg, Virginia, about his father who had wanted him to become an agrarian, while all he'd ever wanted was to become the writer Hemingway was, although he knew he'd have a hard time paring down his prose. He stood up and bowed to Hemingway's portrait at that point, dropping his napkin on the floor, retrieving it, and putting a shirt cuff into the dripping cherry pie while he was at it. It was hard not to like him now since I get food on myself just by looking at it. He discovered I hadn't been to the South yet, and that kept him going over coffee. His large Adam's apple knuckled his throat in rapid succession as he told me how I couldn't possibly begin to appreciate America if I didn't visit the South. He listed the cities I had to see, the universities, the plantations, tempting me with anecdotes for each place.

"You should write a travel book," I suggested, by now completely disarmed.

"I may, I may." He put his cup down and dropped his head in his hand. He stared at me for some uncomfortable seconds, his drooping lock obstructing one eye. "Well, shall we consider the urgent matter at hand? Would you like to go to your apartment where I can tape the interview with a modicum of privacy?"

I looked at the file pinned under his elbow, then back at him. I liked him, a possibility I hadn't considered when I'd set this whole thing up. I couldn't lie to him. And yet I had to help Toni out.

"Listen, Jonathan, I'm not sure about this. I don't really like the gossip business. It can get nasty. I don't mean to put your job down but . . ."

"I hear you and I agree with you completely, but I had to get out of farming the rolling hills of VA in some way, however desperate, which meant I needed a paycheck. This job at least allows me to write. Well, sometimes. Mostly I follow Ms. Gerard around and remind her of appointments and deadlines. I'll be perfectly frank. If you give me this exclusive, I'm in, the road's paved, I can even treat you to the Four Seasons or Lutèce."

"I like it here."

"So do I, so do I. Travel book on the South, hmmmm?" He shifted his head to the other hand. "It's been done, of course, but I could put in excerpts from Eudora Welty, Twain, Faulkner, O'Conner, Williams, Capote, countless others. I'd need great photographs."

"I know just the man."

We paid the bill, which I insisted on sharing even though the magazine would have picked up the tab, and walked up Hudson. I bragged about Toni's photographic talent and ended up confessing the mess he was in. "I know I owe you an exclusive, but I don't know if I can do it. She was murdered, isn't that enough for the public? Why do you have to feed them every unsavory detail? Death is enough of a shocker by itself."

"Then why did you call?"

"Because I need to know if Johanna gave Ms. Gerard an inkling of what the interview was going to deal with. It might be important for Toni."

Jonathan left me on the corner of Bleeker and popped into one of the many rose shops that had mushroomed overnight all over Manhattan. He came out with two white rosebuds: one for me and one for him.

" 'A flower in a buttonhole is the sign of a gentleman,' Gramps used to say. Now they don't make buttonholes, which tells you the state of things." He bent over so I could pin the flower on his lapel. "If I write a basically sweet, nostalgic article about Johanna, will you give me a few details of your own choosing and allow me to use your name? Before you decide, let me confess I know nothing that will be of help to you. The only thing Ms. Gerard wrote down in the Gayle file is 'News that will surprise Hollywood and Rome both!!!!' She really extended herself on the punctuation. The rest is old clippings, list of her films, the usual stuff."

We started walking again, helped by a wind gusting at our backs. "Couldn't Ms. Gerard be keeping it to herself?"

"If so, all is lost. Her memory was gobbled up by our Wang. Seriously, since we've computerized, she types everything into a file and promptly forgets it. A keyboard's the only thing left on her brain."

"Thanks, Jonathan." I extended my hand. We'd reached the Seventh Avenue subway at the corner of Christopher Street. "I know I've been dishonest with you, but I still need to think about the article."

Jonathan seemed to waver in the wind, tall and thin as he was. "Only gentlemanly words will be used, I promise. Unlike Hemingway whose treatment of women is shocking." We shook hands, and I hurried down the subway stairs.

"By the way, Simona," he called out just as I was about to leave daylight behind. "That 'Frying-Fountain-Do' at Lincoln Center was no accident."

"What?"

"Think about that exclusive, OK?"

By the time I ran back to street level, his left Ked was disappearing behind the slamming door of a Yellow Cab. The cab took off, and I was stuck with one more question mark.

Chapter Nine

Sara and Diego were huddled over a flatbed moviola in one of the editing rooms at HearView. The only light in the room came from the one-foot-square screen that flickered a helicopter view of the Statue of Liberty. They were viewing stock footage to use as background for part of the opening credits.

"Linda Shaw will work well," Diego said as I entered, giving me the full benefit of his wide producer shoulders. Sara nodded, marking the frames she wanted with a white editing pencil. She was wearing her rhinestone glasses again, the ones with spikes that covered half her face like a mask.

"We shoot tomorrow at Kennedy Airport." Diego turned on the gooseneck lamp clipped onto the flatbed, while Sara threaded white thread through the frame holes to indicate where her selections were placed in the reel. "Sara has made some judicious cuts that will permit us to fly back to Rome in two days."

"Two days! That's awfully fast," I protested, feeling as if I'd just been thrown on a conveyor belt.

"Don't worry, you will be paid in full."

"Money isn't the only thing people worry about, Diego." How was I going to find out who killed Johanna if everyone disappeared on me? That assistant D.A. was never going to bring the Italian crew back all the way from Italy unless I came up with irrefutable proof that one of them was the murderer. At the rate I was going, there wasn't going to be much chance of that.

"What about Toni?" I practically screamed. "You're just going to abandon him here?"

Diego looked annoyed. "We gave our statements to the D.A. this morning. Toni is in professional hands. There is very little else we can do." He straightened himself up and pushed the rewind button on the moviola. The reel started whistling backwards, Sara's threads whirling into circular white strokes. "Whereas in Italy we will work 48 hours a day if we have to. We have only a month and a half to edit, dub, pull negatives, print, but we must bring the film out for Christmas." His voice was loud, excited. "At the latest New Year's. We must take advantage of the publicity the murder has generated. Everyone will want to see Johanna Gayle's last film." His hand reached out to stop the flapping leader at the beginning of the reel. "This is the one that will do it. This is the film that will bring in all the money we need. That *you* need, Sara, to continue your extraordinary work."

Sara pushed the stop button and turned off the screen light. Something moved behind me and I jumped.

"You make Johanna sound like a cash machine," Massimo said, stepping out of a black corner of the room with his stealthy Mandrake step. "The card of death is slipped in and abracadabra, millions of dollars gurgle out of her." His face, lighted only by the gooseneck lamp, looked white with anger. "Do you have any idea how disgusting you sound?"

"*Santo dio*, Massimo, what do you expect?" Diego asked, stretching out his arms. "I have considered that woman as a business proposition from the very beginning. Did you expect me to think about her pretty legs when I had to pay her the absurd sum of five million dollars? No, no, I accepted her because she was going to make money for me. Now that she is dead, I am going to try to have her make even more money for me. I deal in money, Massimo. I am not in the business of feeling."

"Sara must have a great marriage then."

"Sara knows I love her more than anything in my life." Diego reached for her shoulder and held on to it hard enough to bunch up her shirt.

Sara lifted her glasses with one hand, rubbing her eyes. "It's awful for all of us."

"It isn't awful for any of you," Massimo said in an anguished whisper. "You weren't in love with her, you don't know what it's like to have her hair on your face, to have her whisper, 'you'll take care of me, baby, promise you'll take care of me.' You don't know what's it's like to hold her and never want her to slip away. It hasn't been awful for you because you both hated her! You wanted her dead!" Massimo threw an arm up in accusation. His shoulder hit the light switch behind him. Fluorescent lights popped on. In a film it might have been used as a comic moment. In real life it was embarrassing and awkward. I felt like a Peeping Tom.

Those elaborate rhinestone glasses of Sara's peered up at Massimo. A safety pin jutted out of the left hinge, and just above Sara's eye one of the spikes had a hole the size of a lentil where a rhinestone had dropped out. She would have played the lead clown if her mouth stopped grimacing.

"At heart, aren't you glad she's dead?" she asked in a wearied voice. "You didn't make it this time either. She wasn't going to marry you in Venice or anywhere else. She was quietly letting pudgy little Toni get between her—"

Diego interrupted her with a low, "Sara." She slapped his hand from her shoulder and walked to Massimo.

"You can play bereaved fiancé. You can cry and whimper and lower your eyelids in sadness, and maybe your fans and the press will buy it." Sara pumped the characteristic nervous edge back into her voice, getting louder and louder with each word. "But I'm your director from way back, remember? I can tell the difference between reality and acting. I can always tell!" She shouted now. "I've made a career out of it!" She clasped Massimo's head and started shaking it, then suddenly dropped her hands and hugged him hard. "God, I'm sorry, Massimino, I'm sorry," she repeated.

Massimo patted her back and looked overwhelmed, while Diego pretended to be very busy with cans of stock film. When Sara started telling Massimo how much she loved him, I decided I'd had enough. After one more frantic embrace, she almost dropped her glasses again. I grabbed them before they hit the floor, handed them back, and got out of there.

Raf parked his car on Forty-sixth Street, between Eighth and Ninth avenues, a block known as Restaurant Row because of the plain and fancy eateries crowding each side of the block, ready to stuff the theatergoers. "At least the garbage here smells of garlic," he said, turning off the motor and settling back against the seat. He'd picked me up at HearView ten minutes after I'd left a message for him at the precinct. He said he'd been fast because he happened to be cruising the area. I knew better.

He loosened his tie and gave me a steady, serious Garcia goggle. "Stan is no happy man, Simonita. Wanna tell me what's goin' on?"

"Let's just say I'm trying to become a more emancipated woman, which means that life does not revolve around a man."

"He's a good man, though. Not too quick makin' up his mind in some cases, I'll grant you that. But the best." Raf had been there when Greenhouse and I first met. He felt responsible.

"Listen, Raf, at this point it's got nothing to do with that. First, we both have to make sure what we want in our lives. When we can figure that out, *then* we can talk about who's best for whom."

Raf made a face. "With me and Tina, we need no talkin'. You know what I mean? I looked at

151

her, I liked her, thought she was a great looker. She looked at me, thought I was real cute. I mean she actually told me this right on the first date, that I was real cute, in front of some of the guys. I pump iron till it kills me and she thinks I'm cute. Cute's for sissies. What I mean is, that's it. No complications. We go for each other and one day we're gonna get married." He took my hand. "You know Simonita, it can be simple."

"Neither of you has been divorced."

Raf raised a finger. "You got a point." He reached over in the glove compartment and fumbled with an empty box of tissues, a deodorant spray, and a stack of take-out menus. Finally he found what he wanted. Two Mars Bars. He tossed one in my lap. "Love medicine. Don't go well with the smell of garlic, but it's the best I can do. Unless you wanna go for pizza?"

I shook my head, laughing, feeling tired, even a little teary. The wind that had been whipping around all day was sweeping litter down the street. It had worn me down. So had just a few emotions like Toni's indictment, Tiffany's tears, Massimo and Sara's melodramas. I didn't even want to begin to consider my feelings regarding Greenhouse and my stab at independence. Not with Toni still in trouble. I bit into the candy bar, mentally thanking Raf for his even-keeled temperament and his stock of calories.

"Whenever we're together, we always share food," I mumbled, my teeth stuck with caramel.

"That's what friends do." He tore the wrapper off his bar and bit half off. For a few minutes we just chomped, letting our mouths hang open, loudly sucking at our teeth to free them, helping out with fingers, acting like two teenage kids out to prove nothing. After we'd wiped our hands and our mouths on a Chinese menu, Raf settled back against the car door and looked across the street at Orso Restaurant. "Best garlic pizza in town. Paper thin too. Tina's baby brother works in the kitchen, sometimes brings home the stuff. In my opinion, Linda Shaw's so bleached out she looks like she's been floatin' in the East River for a couple a' weeks. Anyway, Stan's not really seein' her. Not that he tells me any of his private stuff, you know how he is. It's just that I got this feeling here . . ." He stretched his pumped-up torso and gave his stomach a resounding whack, ". . . nothin's there."

"Thanks, Raf, but she's not the real issue." She was nothing compared to ex Irene wanting back, Willy being kept out of my sight, and my feeling only half-alive because a man wasn't nailed into my life. "What did you find out about Sam?"

"Now that guy is someone I can sink my teeth into. *Ehi*, listen, I got Stan's OK on this."

"He doesn't mind?"

"He said you're *loco*. Me, I think he's too pissed off to care. Now why don't you give the guy a call, eh?"

"*Basta*, Raf. Tell me about Sam."

"The guy lied. He's a New Yorker like he told you, but he lived in L.A. for two years. Didn't work for the movies though. He had a small electrical repair shop which he dumped ten years ago, came back here and got a job as a gaffer with NABET through some connections he'd made in

153

L.A. This was all in the police file, by the way."

"Wife, kids?"

"Now bite slowly on this one, 'cause this is hot."

A hand rapped knuckles against the windshield. "Beat it, man, we're keepin' this street clean," a boy said, dropping his face down so he could show off the red beret of the Guardian Angels. He looked all of sixteen.

Raf whipped out of the car and pinned the guy down against the hood before I could blink. "I'm the real thing. *You* beat it!"

I yelled out, "No!" hating that useless violence. Raf released his hold and shook the boy's hand.

"Just be careful next time who you're talkin' to." Raf hiked up his pants, flexed his muscles for show, and got back in the car. The Guardian Angel loped off, the buckles of his boots jangling.

Raf slammed the door. "They think we cops stink, we don't know how to do the job, like we enjoy gettin' killed, right? Shit!" He pummeled the dashboard. "Sorry," he said, after a minute or two, avoiding my eyes. "As I was sayin', Samuel Clark Weston took out a marriage license June 16th, 1981, with a certain Jodi Garter. Much better known as . . ."

"Johanna Gayle. Damn it! That's why he called her 'Jo.' That's why he ripped out those magazine pages of her. That's why she had a fit seeing him at my party. They'd been married!" My hands flew up in the air. "She probably dumped him when she got famous, he's hated and loved her ever since and just maybe killed her with a nice copper wire he kept in his tool kit. This is it, this is it! Toni's going to be—"

"Cohalo con calma." Raf burst out in Spanish, catching my flying hands with his own. *"Calma, Simonita."*

"Why? It makes perfect sense."

He cupped my fingers gingerly, as if he'd caught butterflies. "They did not get married. In no state is there a record of a marriage."

"How about abroad?"

"Sam has no passport." He let go of me then, and I wilted down on the seat.

"I told the D.A.'s office about the marriage license. That rookie jerk in charge of this case was too busy pinning the murder on Toni to have his guys check Sam's testimony."

I perked up. "If he lied, that's bound to help Toni."

Raf's head slowly shifted from side to side as if his thick neck needed oiling. "I don't know. My source in that office says that assistant D.A. isn't listening to no one. He just knows Toni's it." He turned the motor on and coasted down the street.

I thought of what Jonathan had said about the "hot" fountain not being an accident. If he was right, there was a glimmer of hope in that. Maybe. "There's a guy the police should try to find. He's somewhere in Wyoming. Abe, I don't know his last name. Ask Nabet; I can't even get a phone number from them. He might know something about what happened at Lincoln Center that could tie in with the murder."

Raf drove around the block and started cruising east. Slowly, as if he had nowhere to go. " 'Might.' 'Could.' Sounds like we really got somethin' there. Why don't I just quit the police force and come

155

work for you. What's the pay like?"

I laughed. "Never-ending friendship, and my apartment whenever *Mamacita* comes to visit."

"I already got that, boss lady." He winked.

"Thanks for all your help, Raf. Really." Raf rippled a bicep in response. I was about to ask him to get the police description of the man who'd gone up to Johanna's, but looking at the car clock, I decided that was information I could get myself. I didn't want him to throw me out of the car.

Raf drove me to Seventy-second and Broadway, mentioning he was off duty the next day. I was going to be out at Kennedy Airport all day, so I suggested Tina take a sick day in my apartment. I offered to have lunch ready in the fridge.

"You're on, boss lady."

Just as I was getting out of the car, I did have the gall to ask him for a complete list of what was found in Johanna's bedroom. If I decided to do that exclusive for *People,* I needed some details to back me up. I didn't remember much except that damn pillow.

As I started to walk away, I realized there was one more thing I wanted to know.

"This case you and Greenhouse are on, is it dangerous?" Having let go of him heightened my normal fears about his safety for some reason, as if he were more vulnerable without me. In my head I already had him bleeding to death on some sidewalk. Maybe Sara's melodramas were catching on.

"Naw, piece a cake." I got the best Garcia grin. Raf liked my still holding on. "Well, watch them shadows," he said and took off.

I walked the two crosstown blocks to the Majestic. It was five o'clock, close enough to the time Johanna was killed, and I was hoping to ask one Indian employee some questions.

A small man with sunken, dark-rimmed eyes opened the service door and looked at me inquiringly. The name "Mahmoud" was stitched on the pocket of his crisp khaki shirt.

I introduced myself and asked if he'd been on duty the afternoon Johanna was killed.

He sighed. "I cannot answer your inquiry unless you possess police credentials. I regret. I am trying to keep my job, you see," he added in a tone of apology.

I put my palms together in front of my mouth and bowed. *"Nameste, sahib,"* I said, remembering a greeting I'd learned from an Indian film. "On my honor, I am not a reporter. I am here to help a friend."

My attempt at Hindi went over big. "Princes are addressed as *sahib*. I have not yet achieved the status of doorman in this life." He bowed back with a wide smile on his face. "I am simply Mahmoud."

The ice was broken. Mahmoud let me enter a small hallway that smelled of Lysol.

I explained about Toni and told him I needed only two answers from him. How tall was the man he'd let up to Johanna's apartment and did he have an accent? There was no way Toni's speech could pass as American.

He frowned. "All the people have an accent in this city. It is very confusing. Russian, Haitian,

Puerto Rican, Chinese, Korean. Even Irish. Our head doorman comes from Dublin." Mahmoud's English accent was so impeccable he should have been behind the lecture podium of a university, not picking up garbage from the back doors of the rich.

"Try to remember. Did he sound like this?" I strengthened my own accent and tried out a made-up phrase about going up to the nineteenth floor.

"How can I tell? I have been here three months. For me the American accent is as strong as the others. He said very little. Two phrases, no more."

"Do you remember how tall he was?"

"I have told the police that it is difficult to be precise. He wore a hard hat, boots, a large jacket. It is not possible to determine size under those circumstances. I will not testify as to size."

I wanted to be angry at him for being so non-committal, but I couldn't. Starting life over in New York City could make even the strongest lose their footing for a while. Besides, he was being honest about his confusion. Sam seemed to be off the hook. Mahmoud was slender; his wrists looked as breakable as chicken wings. I didn't think he'd forget Sam's lineman's size.

"There was also much commotion with the French lady in 16D," Mahmoud said, again in a gentle tone of apology. "She dropped her necklace, and pearls were rolling down the hallway in a great hurry. She was most unhappy. It was a difficult moment."

Then he might not have noticed. "What about the elevator man?"

"I took him up, all the time hearing French imprecations ring in my ears." He opened the door to let a delivery boy from Zabar's drop off some bags. The smell of fresh onion bagels took over, giving that hallway a quick fix of homey warmth.

"Did you take him down or see him leave?"

"I did not, nor did my replacement. The man removed his outer clothing in the service entrance and left them in Miss Gayle's garbage bin. He must have used her key to come down the fire stairs. They open up in the front lobby. I should have told my replacement he was upstairs, but I did not. Not all the pearls had been found, and I was late for my son's birthday festivities." Deep regret showed on his sunken-cheeked face.

I wasn't feeling much better. Toni still looked like the most likely suspect. "It wouldn't have saved her," I offered as consolation and thanked him for bending the rules. "As far as I'm concerned, you are a prince, *sahib*. In this life and all the ones to come." I didn't get a smile.

As I thought the corner to take the subway, my imagination popped a video in my head to jolt me into thought. The woman in 16D was running wildly after her pearls down a never-ending corridor, screeching *"Mon Dieu! Mon Dieu!"* I ran back to Mahmoud.

"Could it have been a woman?"

His eyes widened. "I would not like to think there is such cruelty in women. In India no woman would do such a thing."

No, I thought, in India some women get burned to death so that their husbands can get a new dowry. I was thinking of Soura. She might be capable of such cruelty if she had a strong motive, but

I couldn't think of any. I doubted she'd gotten to the point of killing actresses because she didn't like their acting. Diego didn't have a motive either. Killing Johanna wouldn't get him his five million back. Besides, sending her on promotional tours around the world was a much surer way of selling movie tickets than promoting her death. That left Sam and Massimo on my list. And Sam was the one who had lied.

"It was perhaps a robber," Mahmoud offered. "Thinking she is very rich," he offered.

"Thinking? She was very rich. That apartment alone must be worth two to three million dollars, and she got five million just for this last film."

Mahmoud hesitated and looked down the empty back hallway. The Zabar bags had been removed, but that homey smell was still hanging on. "Miss Gayle was not rich." He lowered his voice. "She had not paid her maintenance in over six months. The bill is more than fifteen thousand." My chin dropped down to my chest at the news *and* the price. "The board had finally asked her to pay or sell the apartment. She was . . . broken, I believe that is the colloquial expression. No, broke. Miss Gayle was broke."

Like hell she was. What about the five million dollars Diego had paid her?

Chapter Ten

I did some quick shopping for Raf and Tina's lunch the next day and headed home. I'd bought an especially good bottle of white wine, *Gavi dei Gavi*, from Piedmont. After what Mahmoud had told me, Raf was going to have to work a little harder for his new boss lady: on Johanna's finances this time. I walked up the stoop of my building and looked down the street. The trees were a little worse for wear after a day of strong wind; the wisteria on the building next to mine looked straggly and yellow; the sky had turned a deep mauve-gray. It's getting dark earlier and earlier, I thought glumly, suddenly disliking fall because I was going to be without Greenhouse. Hefting up my bags I started fumbling for the keys in my purse. Neither the street lamps nor my hallway light were on so I was proceeding by jagged touch and jingle sound. I cursed out loud for stuffing my entire life in my purse and with a knee hiked the mammoth weight closer. With one hand buried and scrambling, the other clutching two grocery bags, I walked to the front door. From the shadow of the doorway, a hand reached out toward me. I jumped back screaming. My purse and the groceries went flying. For some perverse instinct of self-preservation, I held on to the twenty-four-dollar bottle.

A face peered out into what daylight was left. It was tree-tall Jonathan.

"What the hell do you think you're doing?" I yelled out.

Looking mortified, he immediately crouched down to pick up scattered cans and strewn scallions. "I wanted to help you find your keys. I got your message and came right over. I've been waiting for half an hour."

I'd called his office from HearView, wanting to know more about the "Frying-Fountain-Do" that supposedly hadn't been an accident. "You don't have to lurk in doorways and almost break the most expensive bottle of wine I've ever bought."

With a swoop of his arm, he presented me with a bouquet of scraggly scallions and his own bottle of wine.

"An Oakencroft Chardonnay, pure Virginia grape. I lurked because I was hiding from a churlish Yankee who kept cruising around the block every five minutes staring at me sitting on your stoop. At one point, he demanded to know if I was from the press. I answered with my customary candor and was shown a police badge and told to move on, that you'd gone away." Jonathan was gallantly carrying my shopping bag and his wine while we climbed the stairs. I held on to my *Gavi*.

"Are you in danger?" He sounded excited by the prospect.

I unlocked my apartment door, huffing a little from the scare and the four flights of stairs. "No,

162

I have an overzealous friend." Why didn't Green-house just stay away now that I'd told him to? How was a woman supposed to learn emotional independence if her lover cruised the streets to shoo away her problems? And anyway, Jonathan wasn't a problem at all. He was fun, I decided, as he took two long strides to the kitchen corner and started opening his Virginia grape.

"So why wasn't Lincoln Center an accident?" I asked as I took out two wineglasses from my mini-dishwasher. That's where I store all my glasses and plates — four of each.

"I was watching the shoot from the sidelines," Jonathan said, handing back a filled glass. "I told you I'm a fan of Johanna Gayle. Liz Smith had a blurb about her shooting at Lincoln Center last Sunday, so I went to watch. During that whole fountain scene I was standing right on the drain valve. I even scratched my sole against it. The cable was about a foot away, not on it. So that whole fryathon was made up — a good publicity stunt." Two giant steps and he sat down on the sofa.

I put out some soggy crackers left over from the party and sat on a chair. "Makes sense. The press got there fast enough. I'd call it a cheap stunt, not a good one." I remembered Diego's satisfied smile as the photographers clicked away at Johanna and Sara. The news had made all the papers and the morning TV news. Thanks to Johanna's near miss with death *Where Goes the Future?* had been talked about across the country. It wasn't beyond Diego to pay Abe to put up an act, and Sam might or might not have been in on it. Which didn't help Toni any.

I took a sip of Virginia wine. I didn't like it much, but then I'm wildly nationalistic. I've found fault with an eighty-dollar bottle of *Montrachet* '85. Jonathan looked uncomfortable on my make-shift sofa (two piled-up mattresses): he had to keep his head low because of the loft bed just above, and his knees almost hit his ears. He reminded me of a wooden puppet folded up for the night. He wasn't just fun; he was nice. He didn't deserve to be led on.

"I can't do the exclusive, Jonathan. I'm sorry. I just don't have the stomach for it. I know I lied and I'm sorry. All I did was find the body, call 911, and throw up. If you want to write that up, you're welcome to it. I didn't even like Johanna. I can't go gossiping about her now that she's dead."

The phone rang. Jonathan picked it up since he was practically sitting on it. "Hello?" Jonathan shrugged. "Whoever it was hung up." Half a minute later the phone rang again. This time I quickly reached over the sofa and answered. It was Toni. He'd been the one to hang up, thinking he'd got the wrong number. I caught myself being disappointed.

Toni was going over some stills with Sara at a bar in Times Square. He asked if I wanted to join him. I looked over at Jonathan who'd lifted himself off the sofa and was pretending to be wildly interested in my cookbooks. I didn't want to kick him out. I asked Toni if it was important, if he was OK.

"After keeping you up most of the night, I think you should get some sleep." Hip-gyrating

164

music poured into my ear. "It's Sara's idea to have you come over."

"Tell her I'm too tired. I'm still asking questions, Toni. Don't give up. Something will come up." I purposely didn't tell him about Sam's marriage license or that Tiffany and Bella knew Johanna. I wanted him to stop thinking of Johanna altogether. Not easy when you're accused of her murder.

Sara got on the phone to tell me she missed me, and why didn't I come back to Italy to work for her full time.

"We'll have fun together, I promise." Someone laughed in the background, and Sara laughed back. "I know there's a wild streak in you too. Come home." She sounded drunk. I told her I'd think about it and hung up.

"Bad news?" Jonathan asked. He was taking a sniff of my cinnamon jar.

"Throw that out, will you? I can't stand the smell of it." I wasn't going to be making coffee for Greenhouse for a while. And when and if I did again, he was going to have to drink it without his ex-wife's spicy touch. Jonathan obliged and came back to the sofa.

"No bad news," I said, resisting the urge to retrieve the jar. "Just my director trying to get me back to Italy, which always throws me. I like to think that's all behind me. Listen, how about some dinner? I think I owe you that at least."

"I'd be perfectly happy to take you out." This time Jonathan had stretched himself out. His Keds hit the front door. He looked too comfortable to move.

"I love to cook and I have all the ingredients right here." Raf and Tina would have to forgo the third helping. While I prepared an *insalata u' pisci bbonu*,* a Sicilian "good fish" salad, with corn, scallions, cannellini beans, red peppers, celery, and seared tuna, Jonathan asked me what kept me in the States. I thought it over as I chopped and he opened cans.

"The friendliness of people, I think. Americans support each other. They root for the underdog. In Rome I'd come to feel as if everyone were too cynical or too individualistic to care for anyone else."

"To me it sounds like you're describing New Yorkers."

"There's some of that everywhere I guess, but I'm always amazed at the amount of goodwill there is in this city in the face of crime, disease, poverty. There's an enormous group out there that won't give up. A Roman would just shrug his shoulders and blame it on fate. Too many people over there have given up on improvement, on the possibility of renewal."

"It's all those centuries of incredible history," Jonathan said. "I suppose it can chip your soul."

"I'm not saying that's true with all Italians, but in Rome there was a general air of defeatism that weighed me down. I'd come to the point where I needed a good push to make the most of my life. I feel I get it here. Just think of the help you can get in this country. You name the pain, there's a group out there trying to fix it. I think that's wonderful. It gives such hope!"

*Recipe on page 223

"Are you making the most of your life?" Jonathan asked as he took my bridge table from the closet. Americans also liked to ask very personal questions I'd discovered. I mixed the salad over and over again.

"Let's just say I'm on my way," I said, finally shoving the bowl away.

Jonathan stood the table in front of one of the only two windows of my apartment. "A New York terrace view," he said with a bow, holding a napkin over his arm like a waiter. We set the table and sat down to look out at my half-frozen basil plant on the fire escape. Down on the street two men were singing "She's Got Diamonds on the Soles of Her Shoes" in perfect harmony with Paul Simon. We finished the Virginia grape and the salad and ended our meal with pistachio chocolate-chip ice cream I'd bought for Greenhouse ages ago. Watching Jonathan eat it made me feel like a traitor.

"May I ask you out?" Jonathan asked out of the blue. "Johanna Gayle wouldn't even be mentioned, Scout's honor."

"I'm older than you are."

"I will be thirty in ten and a half months, and dating younger men is the mark of a distinguished woman. Look at Mary McFadden and Mary Tyler Moore." He folded his hands in his lap and gave me a beaming smile. "Besides, if you are older, it's only by a whisper."

"Make it more a six-year-old shouting bout." I was making excuses really. I liked Jonathan. I was even physically attracted to him. But Greenhouse was the one I cared for. Besides, I really did want

167

to have a male-free period. "I'm a little confused right now about men in general. Maybe we can think about it when this murder case is over, and Toni's off taking pictures at Les Seychelles or something."

Jonathan leaned over and kissed my forehead. "I will certainly think about it. From this instant. And I want to talk to Toni about the Southern book, if I may. I called a friend of mine over at Stewart, Tabori and Chang. They'd like to hear more."

I applauded. Finally, a bit of American hope for Toni too; something to think about besides jail and a dead Johanna. "He could feast on American breakfasts for three months. Grits and all."

Jonathan got up and picked his tweed jacket off the sofa. "Thank you for the food, which was excellent. It is my habit to help with the dishes, but frankly I'm too disappointed to hang around."

I walked to the door and opened it for him. "I apologize for the missing exclusive. It was very unfair of me."

He shut the door with a snap. "I don't give a damn about the exclusive!"

His face bent over me. For a few seconds I felt very desired, and I was tempted to let him kiss me. I turned my head in time.

"God, I almost forgot!" Jonathan said, straightening up and flapping his arms awkwardly. "Ms. Gerard called the office from L.A. this afternoon. I managed to pry something out of her memory bank that might be of interest. Johanna told her the interview was going to be a confession of sorts. She said something about finally having found happiness and the courage to deal with certain things. Is that any help?"

I stood on my toes and kissed his chin. "Every little bit helps."

As soon as Jonathan left, I wondered if that new-found happiness had anything to do with Toni. I was tempted to call Bella and ask her about Johanna, but the thought of getting Tiffany into trouble stopped me. There would have to be an indirect way to approach Bella. I turned the eleven o'clock news on. Chuck Scarborough, in his mild sweet way, mentioned Toni's indictment. Then the gloating face of John O'Grady, the assistant D.A., appeared above a flock of craning microphones.

"The right man's been indicted, no doubt about it," he said, looking straight into the camera. "Like some guy said, Hell hath no fury like an Italian scorned."

I got him right between the eyes with my shoe, cracking the TV set.

Chapter Eleven

At seven in the morning a 747 Alitalia jet gleamed in the abandoned strip of runway to which the Port Authority had banished us for that day's shoot. A crew member was driving a lawn mower across the surrounding grass to make the strip look less forsaken. A few other members picked up litter, trailing green plastic bags shaped like whales. At one edge of the runway, a cluster of reporters was being asked to leave by hired security guards. Sara had declared the set closed, which meant no spectators allowed. The enforcement of this rule had nothing to do with Johanna's death. We were shooting the last scene of the film, and the endings of Sara's films were always well-kept and much-gossiped-about secrets. Crew and actors were sworn to a silence they gladly kept. Movie sets can have their own brand of *omertà,* that Mafia-like loyalty that guarantees future work.

The day was hot and gorgeous, postcard-blue sky, throbbing yellow sun — pure Indian summer magic. I had practically no work to do. The day's dialogue was an awkward, but pregnant "There's no more time, Your Excellency," spoken by one of the Alitalia hostesses, and a "Gianni, Gianni" yelled by Linda Shaw. Massimo had a lot of dramatic emoting to do with his mouth blessedly shut. A dialogue coach's dream day, except for the fact that I had to keep my jaw going with a few questions that needed answers. I started with the easier target.

Makeup and Wardrobe were in a hangar two hundred feet from the shooting site. I weaved through single engine planes that looked like a boy's idea of the perfect Christmas, trying to spot Massimo and Linda Shaw. I had no desire to look upon her beautiful face, much less hear her enthusiasm. Luckily, Massimo was sequestered in a corner a good twenty feet away from the others. He sat under a wide band of dusty sunlight that cut down from long horizontal openings high on the hangar wall. A mirror propped up on a chipped Formica desk reflected his face in my direction. Starched white napkins ruffled around his neck like a stiff Elizabethan collar. He looked fast asleep while his faithful makeup man patted his face into a vigorous virile tan. I walked up quietly and sat down on a stool to wait. The makeup man started snipping hairs from Massimo's nose. Massimo's tongue flicked behind a cheek. He was awake.

"I spoke with the *People* reporter who was going to interview Johanna," I said in a bored, offhand way. His hand twitched.

"I called him thinking he might know something that would help Toni."

Massimo waved his makeup man away and tore the napkins from his neck. "These goddamn things make me itch. Well, did he know something?" He palmed his hair in the mirror, trying to look as if he didn't care. He wouldn't have won any Oscars on this one.

"What was Johanna going to say that scares you so much?" I asked. Direct questions American-style were becoming a habit with me.

He shook his head slowly with a smile, using his poise to smooth the moment. " 'Scared' is such a dramatic, hyperbolic word. 'Curious' is more apropos. Johanna was sometimes a little spoiled, insensitive. You saw that yourself with that silly scene she made over Sam being at your party. It doesn't really matter now. She never gave that interview." He looked at me with raised eyebrows, expecting me to confirm. I told him I had to find the actress playing the airline hostess and left him following my exit in his propped-up mirror. He wasn't going to be the only one playing games.

I walked back on the runway, looking for Sam. Sara was talking to the DP under a green-and-white café umbrella advertising San Pellegrino bottled water. The camera basked in the shade of an identical umbrella speared into the grass embankment. Grips were laying down dolly tracks leading to the left wing of the plane. A new still photographer was snapping shots of anything that moved. I watched him go down on one knee and aim his Nikon upward at the Goodyear blimp slugging through the sky like a bloated fish. I found myself missing Toni terribly.

Sam stood on the metal stairway propped against the First Class doorway, where the prime minister was going to enter the plane. His Rams-capped head was bent over his chest, reading his light meter. I went up the stairs. He saw me coming and tipped the visor of his cap closer to his nose.

"Why don't you tell your pizzaland director that in the U.S. we use jetways to get into a 747, not these rickety stairs."

"The ending of the film wouldn't be quite as dramatic shot in a narrow, dark corridor, don't you think, Sam?" I took one step closer. "I saw those pictures in the bathroom."

He looked up, the visor of his cap shading his eyes. "Mind your fucking business."

"I am not going to, not with Toni going on trial. Why didn't you marry her?" He lunged down two steps, then stopped himself. I clung to the railing, knowing I didn't have a chance if he wanted to shove. He stood looking at me for an eternity, then abruptly pushed past, his shoulder hitting my head.

I followed him to one of the green-and-white umbrellas where the DP started giving him instructions for the setup of the lights. Linda Shaw, dressed to explode a man's arteries in a tight-fitting Calvin Klein bare beige silk shirt and skirt, walked toward us, waving at me. I had nothing to hide behind as she came running to my side.

"You're Simona, right? I can't thank you enough. I hear I owe it all to you. This is so much fun." She had more of a corn-fed look than Johanna, with a confident, warm smile. "It beats giving aerobics classes for eight hours a day."

"I'm sure," I muttered politely. She seemed nice, but she made me think of Greenhouse and I wanted him out.

"I hope I didn't do anything taboo, Simona." The wind picked up her hair and lashed it to one side of her face. They had lightened it and taken the curl out to match Johanna's. "I was so excited about being in a movie, and I told a young friend he could come over and watch the shoot. That's OK, isn't it?"

I thought about the word "young." Greenhouse was forty. No way would that pass for young in this country. Especially not coming from a woman who hadn't hit the three zero mark yet. "It's a closed set today. I'm sorry they didn't warn you."

"Oh, that's terrible. He's only thirteen, and he was thrilled at the idea of seeing an Italian gangster movie being made. What should I do? It's too late to stop him. He's the son of a really good friend of mine, you know, and I kind of wanted to please both of them."

Great! Dear Miss Shaw had invited Willy to the set. Just what I needed. "When he comes, let me know. I'll see that he gets to peek from the hangar. Just make sure Sara doesn't spot him."

"Thanks, that's really nice of you."

I wasn't being nice; I was curious. I'd get to meet Willy finally. And maybe I'd find him really obnoxious and I'd be glad I had no part of him. I nodded and walked off after Sam.

He was back on the metal stairway taking a light reading on Massimo. Sara was at the foot of the stairs talking to a man dressed in rags, his long burlap-colored hair matted down with dirt. As I came closer, I recognized the Times Square man to whom Massimo had offered his shoes.

"Hey there, remember me?" I asked him, proffering a hand. He picked up the tip of his coat and curtsied, a wide grin on his face.

"Course I do. As I always say, my business is

174

noticin'. I never forget a face or a pair of shoes."
He lifted a leg to show me a brand-new pair of
black leather boots. "That good man got me a
day's job." He pointed to Massimo four steps
above him. "But this lady here wants me to take
my new shoes off, finds them too handsome for
the purpose of this film. She wants me barefoot. I
tell her she's discriminating against the homeless."

Sara threw up her hands in despair. She was
wearing narrow, black wrap-around sunglasses,
black tights and an oversize T-shirt that made her
look as if she were in mourning. Until she turned
around. Across her back, white block letters announced that ITALIANS DO IT BETTER.

Sara had a barefoot beggar appear in the most
unlikely places in all her films. In one film, the
beggar had walked across a bedroom during a tor-
rid love scene between the protagonists. In another, he had sat on a pulpit, dirty feet dangling
above the open mouths of Catholics about to re-
ceive Holy Communion. The beggar's presence was
meant to jar Sara's public out of the story for a
few seconds, to remind them that human need was
always present.

"You are very important to my film," she told
the Times Square man in a coaxing tone. "Your
face will end the film."

"My face?"

"*Si, si,* your face."

"What's my face got to do with my shoes?"

I ran off before Sara started screaming for me
to solve the problem. Sam was ahead of me, hurrying toward one of the equipment trucks. "Come
on, Sam, you liked Toni," I yelled. He stopped to
plug in some connectors.

I walked up to him, making sure other crew members were close enough to us just in case Sam got the urge to kick me over the runway for a field goal. "What's the teamster's alphabet?" I asked. Sam ignored me. "Fuckin' A, fuckin' B, fuckin' C." I crouched down beside him. "You told Toni that joke. You drank beers together. Come on, you almost married the woman. Maybe you know something about her that can help." He was still pretending he was deaf.

"What really happened at Lincoln Center, Sam? Can you at least tell me that?"

"Sam, are you ready?" the DP yelled out. Sam stood up slowly and looked down at me, his beer belly taking up most of the view from my vantage point.

"Nothin' happened at Lincoln Center. I saved her just in time so your friend could kill her off!"

I stood up. "The nicked cable wasn't anywhere near the drain valve."

Sam ran a thumb inside his belt line and walked off, his shoulders and arms held out as if he were ready to tackle anything that came his way. I was lucky he hadn't bopped me one. I watched him as he loosened a light stand on one side of the dolly track. He climbed a ladder and pulled a scrim that was reducing the light of an HMI and gave the DP the thumbs-up sign. Sam too thought Toni was the killer. Suddenly I felt like Sisyphus in Hell vainly trying to roll that huge stone up the hill.

Sara called *"Azione!"* and I stood by, glad to be distracted by a movie in the making.

145. EXT. JFK RUNWAY. DAY.

CAMERA follows PRIME MINISTER as he walks toward the waiting 747 ALITALIA jet. Behind him JOURNALISTS follow until they are stopped by an AIRPORT OFFICIAL. CAROLE is among them, her back to the camera. PRIME MINISTER stops, lets his ENTOURAGE get ahead of him and slowly turns toward CAROLE.

DOLLY TO:

CLOSE-UP of PRIME MINISTER looking at CAMERA. A swarm of emotions hover over his face. He is tempted to stay with his passionate love, Carole. If he does not board the plane, not only will he destroy his family back in Italy, but the ensuing scandal might make him lose his post as Prime Minister. He would forgo the possibility of stopping the Red Brigades' assassination attempts. Ambition wins out. He drops his eyelids and gives a light, forgiveness-seeking smile. Then he lifts his hand to his mouth and opens his palm toward the waiting journalists. It is his good-bye kiss to Carole.

DOLLY BACK TO:

INCLUDE PARTIAL VIEW of plane's left wing. A luggage carrier, piled high with suitcases, can be seen stopping under the shade of the wing. DRIVER reaches behind his

seat. AIRLINE HOSTESS approaches
PRIME MINISTER.

> AIRLINE HOSTESS
> There is no more time, Your Excellency.

PRIME MINISTER turns around and begins
to walk up stairway.

145A. EXT. DAY. DOLLY TO:

PROFILE of CAROLE noticing the luggage
carrier. A look of horror appears on her face.
She pushes AIRPORT OFFICIAL out of her
way and runs toward the plane.

> CAROLE
> Gianni! Gianni!

FOUR SECURITY GUARDS posted on the
stairway pull out their guns. CAROLE points
under the wing.

145B. EXT. DAY. CUT TO:

MEDIUM SHOT of luggage carrier DRIVER.
His face is hidden by a cap worn low on his
forehead. He is pointing a rifle left of camera, finger on the trigger. Shots ring out. A
woman's scream is heard off camera. CAM-
ERA CLOSES IN on DRIVER's lap, revealing two thick stumps that had once been legs.
They are splattered with blood. Wounded
DRIVER re-aims rifle and pulls the trigger.

CAROLE doubling over and falling at the
foot of the stairway. PRIME MINISTER tries
to reach her, but is stopped by his SECU-
RITY GUARDS, who hustle him up the steps
and into the plane. AIRPORT SECURITY
and JOURNALISTS crowd around
CAROLE's body.

Sam and I were standing to the left of the
traveling camera, not ten feet from Linda.
Throughout the first take, he held a grip stand
against the wind, looking as sturdy as an oak, his
eyes set on the horizon. Sara declared the take
perfect and asked for one more, for safety. Linda
went through her bit again: clutching a second,
clean shirt at the sound of the rifle shot, pressing
open a new plastic sac of fake blood hidden between her breasts, falling on her stomach like a
pro (her gymnastic training came in handy), careful to knock hair over her face so that the camera
wouldn't pick up the fact that she wasn't Johanna.
When Linda hit the asphalt this time, she let out
a moan. Sam looked down as the blood oozed out
and spread into a large puddle that dyed the tips
of Linda's hair a deep pink. Sam turned green and
wavered. I put my arm out to steady him. Not
that I could have held him if he'd gone down.
Linda lay there on the sticky asphalt, playing dead
and looking like Johanna's twin.

"She was the most beautiful thing I ever held,"
he said after a deep breath. He turned so he could
no longer see Linda. His gaze was now fixed on
the wing tip. "She stood me up. I waited and

waited outside her apartment that morning. We were going to drive to Big Sur and get married at Nepenthe." He was whispering even though the mike was far away and probably picking up coughs of wind. "She wanted it to be romantic."

Sara called "cut," and everyone started moving at once as if she'd pushed the forward button. Sam stayed put, holding on to his wavering grip stand.

"She was just an unhappy kid then, looking to break into the movies. Nineteen years old. I didn't know about her rich father or anything about her. Except that she was scared most of the time. Sometimes she'd just ask me to hold her. 'Make it go away,' she'd tell me. Christ, I never even made love to her. She wanted to be a virgin on her wedding night, and that was just fine with me as long as I was the one marrying her."

Luckily, the DP and Sara left us alone. Sam's assistants set up the lights for the next shot without him.

"How'd you meet?" I asked.

"A busted electric stove. She didn't have the money to pay me. She kept calling up and apologizing. It went from there. Three great months, then outta my life she went."

A gigantic HMI, barn doors flapping in the wind like frantic wings, wheeled past us. Sam woke up to his duties and started giving orders. I followed him, unwilling to let his gregarious moment pass.

"Do you know why she changed her mind?"

"Her father found her. He took her back to New York, gave her dancing, singing, acting lessons. Whatever she wanted. I got a note about a month after the wedding date saying I was to forget she existed."

The DP interrupted with last-minute instructions. Sam went back and forth between equipment truck and the stairway with perspiring, squinting me in tow. Sam's lights were merciless, and the sun was strong despite the wind that came and went. The plane squatted on the runaway, silver turning into white, reverberating waves of heat.

We stopped by the truck one more time. "Didn't you try to contact her?" Sam picked up a wrench and threw it inside the bowels of the truck. It struck metal with a sharp cracking sound. It was clear he was angry. At me for gnawing at him or at Johanna?

I followed him back to the green-and-white umbrella that was shielding the camera. It was time to shoot again.

145C EXT. DAY. CUT TO:

CLOSE UP of the back of CAROLE's head. A pair of feet, caked with dirt and scabs, walks into frame and stops next to her bloodied hair. After a few seconds, they walk away, leaving footprints in a pool of blood.

CAMERA DOLLIES BACK to show an empty runway with beggar walking away toward the horizon, his long coat flapping in the wind. Dark smudges of blood trail behind him. FREEZE FRAME. END CREDITS ROLL.

We broke for lunch and I doggedly persisted. I wasn't forgetting that Johanna had accused him of

181

stalking her.

"Johanna became a famous actress, and you came to New York and got yourself a movie job." I bit into a sandwich. Mayonnaise and tuna oozed down my shirt front. I was too nervous to care. "Were you hoping to meet up with her on the set? Or off the set?" I looked around to make sure I was surrounded by actors and crew members. "Maybe you were furious with her and wanted to settle accounts?"

Sam lit a cigarette and ran his thumb inside the belt line of his jeans again. "Who's to say?"

"The police know about the marriage license, Sam."

"What do the police know?" Massimo asked in Italian, walking up behind me. He'd taken off his gray prime minister's jacket and covered himself with a garish red silk kimono. He wore a net on his head to protect his thinning hair from the wind. He looked ridiculous and his timing stank.

"Sam and I are having a private conversation."

"Exactly what I need from you. *Pardon*, Sam." Massimo wrapped his arm around my shoulders and steered me away.

"Much obliged," Sam yelled after him. "And watch out, she'll get you talking straight to the electric chair."

"What does he mean by that?" His voice was trembling, and his face looked pasty under the melting pancake makeup.

"Just one of Sam's jokes." The wind rose at that moment, wrapping my skirt around my legs, pushing me against Massimo. Scrims and nets started skimming across the asphalt. Grip stands toppled over. A green-and-white umbrella lifted up for a moment of flight, then capsized like a felled mushroom. Massimo gripped my shoulders as the wind blew his hair net away. "Did Johanna say anything to that reporter?" He squeezed. "Did she?"

"Hey, stop it, you're hurting me." Massimo relaxed his grip.

"Did she?"

"I don't know. Why? What are you afraid of?"

Massimo let go of me and threw his barely smoked cigarette on the runway. The wind picked it up and played cat and mouse. Massimo shivered. *"Niente.* Nothing, except that Johanna was so unpredictable. She was capable of saying a lot of nonsense."

So are you, I thought. "Actually, Johanna had a preliminary chat with *People.* All I know is that she was going to give them news that would surprise Hollywood and Rome. With three exclamation marks." I rubbed my burning shoulders.

"She's a sick woman," Massimo said. "Very sick. If she says anything about me, I'll tell the world about her." He'd momentarily forgotten she was dead, it seemed. "I'll be the one who'll shock Hollywood and Rome."

A real gentleman, Macho Man Massimo turned out to be. He was sickening enough to make me mean. "The reporter is a friend of mine. I'll let you know what more I find out." I was convinced Johanna hadn't told *People* anything else. I just wanted to make Massimo sweat a little.

"Che cazzo fai, Massimo?" Sara's voice punched my ear, nearly knocking my head sideways. "Get over to Makeup. We're shooting your close-up in five minutes. And you, Simona, should know bet-

ter." She stomped her boot heel and looked unpleasant. Behind her, Diego raised his eyebrows.

What I should know better I had no idea, but I bowed demurely to the boss while Massimo scampered off toward the hangar, pursued by Wardrobe trying to flag him down with a dark gray suit jacket.

Diego bestowed two polite pecks on my cheeks, a first in our relationship, and together we watched Sara stride back toward the camera, dragging the heels of her lizard boots like a sullen child.

"Our departure tomorrow comes not a day too soon." Diego kept his hands in his pockets and jingled coins. "Massimo's nerves are fraying, and my sweet Sara has not been easy to live with. Looking at the back of her T-shirt today, I ask myself what it is that we Italians actually do better." He half-turned toward me, showing surprising enthusiasm on his face. "Survive, I suppose. We shall do that quite nicely, I believe."

I must have made a face because he quickly wiped the smile off his lips. "I am not heartless, Simona. *La signorina* Gayle was a nice woman and a good actress, but she was also difficult and very rude to Sara. That did not predispose me well toward her."

"What didn't predispose you well was the five million dollars you had to give her." Diego stiffened, stopping that loose change racket. Had he given the money to her? Maybe not, and that was why Johanna had started making a fuss on the set. It was Diego who had come to the rescue that night at Lincoln Center. He had walked in calmly, in perfect command of the situation. She had

184

fluffed her hair, hardly an angry gesture. But then she may not have wanted me to know the humiliating fact that she hadn't been paid. I looked at Diego who had produced a tight, reconciliatory smile on his square-jawed face. Five million dollars was a very good reason to kill for a man as constantly worried about money as he was.

"Finding Linda Shaw was an extraordinary coup for which the production is forever indebted to you," Diego said. "There will be a bonus in your paycheck that should be generous enough to mollify your harsh opinion of me." With that he swept a cashmered shoulder under my nose and walked away.

What opinion did I have of him, I wondered. I hadn't given Diego much thought before. It was hard with Sara around. She was always firmly center frame, and he did nothing to butt in. If he was money-hungry, it was for her. I needed to know if that five million had ever changed hands to decide what I really thought of Diego. Raf would clear that up for me by the end of the day, I hoped. I'd pinned a note on my pillow asking him to do this one last favor. If Johanna never got the money, I might have found her murderer.

Linda Shaw waved from the distance of the hangar, the bloodied front of her shirt bright enough to flag a bull. She was doing a very bad job of hiding a lanky boy in an equally bright green Jets jacket. Green, Greenhouse's favorite color.

I walked slowly, trying to relax. Linda and Willy disappeared inside the hangar. When I got there, he was gawking at a red-and-white single-engine plane, stroking one side as if it were the flank of a beloved horse.

"Hi," I called out, anxious to sound cheerful and welcoming. He turned around. I stopped walking. The lanky boy in front of me did not have the blue eyes nearly hidden by thick, corn-silk lashes in the photo that I had probed in Greenhouse's wallet. This boy had the same blond hair, the requisite American freckles, but his eyes were the color of roasted chestnuts. I wasn't sure whether I was relieved or disappointed.

"Joey, meet Simona," Linda said. "His dad and I are planning to get married. Joey said it's all right with him that I come live with them. Isn't that right, Joey?" Linda laughed with what seemed embarrassment, and Joey didn't look at all convinced. So much for my assumptions and suspicions, I thought, feeling a hot flash of anger. When was I going to stop jumping to conclusions and thinking the worst whenever I came up with something I didn't immediately understand? When was I going to stop leaving my brains on the pasta plate?

I showed Joey around the hangar, introduced him to various crew members, describing what each of them did. When Massimo's close-up was shot, I explained Joey's presence to Sara, and she gave him a sudden hug, offering to buy the Jets jacket off his back for two hundred dollars. I gave up trying to understand Sara's reactions and went off to use the phone.

Toni's defense lawyer was in court, but his secretary assured me in a Vaseline-thick murmur that any message I left with her would be delivered. I told her briefly about Sam's relationship to Johanna, about the supposed state of Johanna's finances in case the lawyer hadn't looked into that yet, and gave her my telephone number in case he wanted to reach me. Then I called home hoping Raf or Toni would answer. They didn't, and I tried working my answering machine long distance. For some crazy reason it worked. I got a strangely subdued message from Raf letting me know that lunch was great, and that he'd put the cinnamon jar that he'd found in the garbage right back on the kitchen shelf. He'd gone back to the precinct to try to find out about "the money shortage," and his source in the D.A.'s office had let slip that Abe was on a flight back to New York. When Raf had asked for explanations, the source had clammed up.

No one answered my call at Bella's or Tania's. For all I knew, Toni was in the East River.

The only shot left for the day was a pan across the Alitalia logo on the side of the plane. It was one of Diego's many money-saving deals. For a few minutes of promised exposure, Sara, Diego, the DP, and the two leads had flown first class on the house. No actors were involved with the shot, so I asked Sara's permission to leave.

"Where'll you be?" she asked after offering me a production car.

"At my place or the B and B." I wanted to see Toni.

Chapter Twelve

By the time the production car drove me to SoHo, it was almost six o'clock. Clouds had appeared in pink-orange streaks to soak in the last of the sun. I got out at Houston, SoHo's northern border, and walked past the fancy shops and art galleries of West Broadway down to Bella's.

Tiffany let me in, holding a pair of nail scissors in her hand. Bella had gone to "group," and Tiffany hadn't seen Toni since she'd been back from school. I asked her if I might wait for him or her mom. She gave me a penetrating seven-year-old look to decide if I was friend or foe. Friend won out.

"Are you giving yourself a manicure?" I asked as she made way for me to come in. "I'm very good at hand massage and nail polish."

"I'm not allowed to touch big scissors." Tiffany turned around and went to her room, closing the door behind her. So much for friendly conversation. The kitchen table was again covered with dirty breakfast and lunch dishes. I cleared and started washing to wile away time and save Tiffany the job later. Then I began feeling bad about the door she had closed in my face. I walked along the Pompeian red plasterboard wall and knocked at her door.

"May I come in, Tiffany? I really am sorry I made you cry yesterday. Will you forgive me?"

She opened the door, her thin face as solemn as before, and slipped back to her desk. She resumed her work, brushing glue on the back of a newspaper sheet she'd cut into a long oval. She sucked her lower lip in concentration as she swept the small brush in long uneven strokes. Her other hand, fastening the clipping flat against the desk, got covered with licks of glue.

"I want that blue paper." Tiffany pointed to a bookshelf to her left. I picked up the thick sheet and handed it over. Tiffany turned her newspaper oval around, neatly placing it at the center of the stiff blue sheet. The heel of one hand smoothed Johanna's front-cover photo from last Monday's *Post*. Sara's face peeking from the limousine window had been cut out, and the only thing left of Diego was a snipped-off arm around Johanna's shoulder.

Tiffany examined her work by distancing herself and squinting her eyes, as she might have seen Bella do in front of one of her own canvases.

"You did a good job," I said. "We've got lots of pictures of Johanna that Toni took for the film that you can have. Just of her. Big, small, black and white, color, whatever you want."

She smiled then and raised her arms. "This tall. In color. For the back of my door."

"Done." We were friends again.

"Thank you for washing the dishes and knocking on my door," Tiffany said as she stuck Johanna on the inside of her closet door with a thumbtack. "Mom never does."

Her words slipped in, made contact, and there I was with a replay in my mind. Johanna's trailer. She and I talking. The door opens and Diego's polite baritone voice interjects. The door opens.

That was the point. He hadn't knocked.

I knelt down and picked up strips of newspaper from the floor. I found Diego's one-armed photo and held it up. "Do you know this man?"

Tiffany sucked in both her lips and nodded slowly.

"Did he come here with Johanna?"

"I don't like him."

"Why not?"

"He made her cry," Tiffany said. Sitting on her bed, she put a hand, fingertips crusty with glue, against the wall. "I listened right through here. It wasn't like with Mom and her boyfriends."

So they were lovers. A familiar hollow in my stomach faintly echoed the past pain of my own two-timing husband. It was just a second of distraction.

"Johanna cried or she made funny noises, like a mouse. When they get caught in that gluey stuff, they squeak a lot." Tiffany looked at the glue crusts on her hands and pressed her fingers together. Then she slowly opened them, maybe to check they didn't stick. "He asked her to marry him."

Diego and Sara were not a happy couple at all. Diego was in love with Johanna just like Sam, Massimo, Toni. Diego was a hypocrite, a liar.

Tiffany started biting the glue from her thumb. "She was going to leave New York with him. She was real happy."

I took her hand from her mouth. "That stuff can make you sick."

Tiffany got up and went to wash her hands in the bathroom next door. She left the door open, and I could sea her Mondrian shower curtain. It was the best thing her mother had painted in that loft. "When was the last time you saw them together?"

Tiffany dried her hands on the blue pleated skirt of her school uniform and came back to her room. "Tuesday. They came real early and shut themselves up in the room. I played sick and didn't go to school. She laughed a lot."

Tuesday, the day of the murder.

"I didn't want her to go away, but she said she had to, and she said that one day the right man would come for me, and I would be happy and go away too." How solemn Tiffany looked, trying very hard to be grown-up. "I don't want to go away. I don't want anyone to go away." She opened her blue eyes wide, as if something had caught inside, then started blinking fast. I thought of Willy, of how lucky he was his father was still around and cared so much.

I offered to play a game. Tiffany preferred to show me the jewelry she'd collected from Johanna and other guests. She had quite a collection of trinkets in a pink, fake leather box that she kept locked in her closet. I paid attention to her muttering identifications, making appreciative mumbles, slipping an arm around her thin waist, tucking in her school blouse, smoothing her hair. She let me fuss over her, and I became acutely aware of her loneliness and mine. At the same time I couldn't help thinking of Sara. Did she know about Diego? I slipped Diego's cutout into the waste paper basket, noticing his square-jaw, the same look of stern authority I'd seen in the photograph of Johanna's father in her living room. Diego-Daddy, had that been the appeal?

Tiffany took out her "second to best thing," Johanna's locket being "the very best ever." It was a gaudy, looped rhinestone necklace Bella had given her that I immediately hated. It was ugly and vulgar. I had a hard time not tearing it out of Tiffany's hand and throwing it in the waste basket. That necklace was typical of Bella, I thought. Typical of a mother who let lovers sleep next to her daughter's room, who made enough noise with her own boyfriends to allow her child to distinguish between happy and unhappy love sounds. I was uncomfortable and angry. Sara's gaunt, wrinkled face peered up from these thoughts. She had to know, I realized. It couldn't have been a coincidence that she suggested Toni hide out in Bella's B&B.

When the pink jewelry box had been emptied and filled again, Tiffany said she needed to do her homework, asking me not to say anything to Mom because "that man" gave Bella money not to tell anyone.

"My Dad forgets to send money. Mom says we need whatever we can get."

I kept a straight face and went to call Raf at the precinct. He was on the phone, and I left Bella's number for him to call me back. In the meantime I went to gather Toni's things. I wasn't about to let him stay in the same place Johanna and Diego had made love. That was something he didn't need to find out about ever. If he saw Tiffany's cutout of Johanna, he might start putting things together and get drowned out by more pain. He was much better off staying at Tania's, media or no media. Besides, no reporters had called at my place except for Jonathan.

Raf returned my call after about ten minutes. Johanna had gotten paid after all. The five million was in the Kemper Market Fund. In late June she had mailed in Diego's check for two and a half million. The last two and a half had been put in on Monday, the day before she died. Payments were made by V&V Productions according to her contract.

"The woman had less than two thousand in her bank account. Her father's securities *desaparecido*. She was a big spender. Looks like she owed half the city, but she didn't touch those mills. Maybe she was finally getting tight."

I had my opinion of Diego now: a two-timing bastard with no motive for murder. I was back to zero. "Thanks Raf, you're an angel."

"I'm an angel not to tell Stan about that cinnamon. That almost pissed me off. I mean you don't throw a guy in the garbage without a hearing."

"It's only a jar, Raf." God, I didn't need to get into this now.

"*Simbólico,* Simonita. Don't try to kid Rafael Garcia. *Simbólico.*" He was beginning to sound like Sara.

Bella finally showed up. I had nothing to say to her except that I didn't think Toni was coming back, so I was taking his things. I offered to pay for that night, but she said she was sure that "nice Italian gentleman," meaning Diego, would settle the bill. Tiffany came out to say good-bye, and I promised to add to her jewelry collection. Downstairs I stuck a note for Toni on the doorknob of the front door and headed home.

A block away, at the corner of Mercer, Jonathan's face peered out through an etched glass window of Fanelli's Café. Seeing me, he knocked on the pane and gestured for me to come in. Toni's red head popped up and smiled.

The buzz of the place was surprisingly low. The crowd wasn't the slick group clad in bat-black that descended on SoHo by night. These were earthy resident regulars, dressed with whatever they found quickly that morning, paint, clay, or sawdust still clinging in the creases of clothes and skin. One old man on the corner stool sent off a calming smoke-stained rumble that quit only for long sips of foaming ale. He looked as if he'd been around, bending the bartender's ear since the founding of the place back in 1873. Pleasant ghosts were probably muttering in other corners. I'd come back here, I decided, when I was in a better mood to listen.

"What are you two doing together?" I said, sitting down in a chair facing the long wooden bar. I gave Toni a kiss and a hug. Jonathan got a neutral handshake.

"I stalked him until I found him," Jonathan said. "We're in the neighborhood to pick up his stuff." His bow tie — blue polka dots on yellow silk — was untied, and his button-down collar was open to give free range to his large Adam's apple. His eyes were shining. "Toni was doing fire escapes. He must have shot ten rolls of West Village fire escapes. He's my photographer. Yes, ma'am. Totally dedicated to the capturing of an image." Jonathan grinned happily.

"I want to do the book," Toni said, picking up on Jonathan's smile. "Even as a try."

"On spec," Jonathan corrected.

"That's what I said." Toni laughed. His nose and cheeks were red, and I suspected he'd had one too many, but who cared? It was wonderful to hear him laugh again.

"Simona finds the true killer, and I go take photographs of Mardi Gras. Good idea, no?"

"Great idea," I said, refusing the drink Jonathan offered. I was a lousy detective; I was spinning around in circles; I'd uncovered ugly, painful intimacies that were no help at all; I was tired. I wanted out.

I kicked Toni's bag against his ankles and told him to come sleep at Tania's apartment. "The only reporter I've seen is Jonathan, so you're safe."

Jonathan pushed a lock of hair off his forehead. "Thanks to that man in blue, no reporter can stay near your apartment. 'Man in blue' is a euphemism for any Yankee. That he's a policeman makes that particular nomenclature all the more appropriate. He was cruising by again tonight. Possessive S.O.B., isn't he?" He downed a neat shot of vodka. "As I explained to Toni," he said, smacking his lips, "not all Southerners drink mint juleps. Nor are we all gentlemen." He gave me a bleary, sad smile. "I hate rejection in any form." I played with a coaster, understanding exactly how he felt.

Jonathan then offered to put Toni up at his place in Brooklyn. Toni said yes, then looked at me guiltily. I told him it was fine with me, that he should think of it as a vacation from the old Italian gang. He looked grateful. They were probably going to drink themselves into a stupified dream: Berto & Frey, the international photo/word geniuses waving to the crowd from the heights of publishing Olympus. Why not? I might have eaten myself into a similar daze if I hadn't been so tired.

By the time I left Fanelli's, it was dark out and the day's warmth had worn off. I shivered, wanting a sweater, and headed north. Mercer was deserted except for a woman staring out of a black-and-white TV in an otherwise empty gallery window. As I hurried by, she asked, "Are you bothered by the fact that I am black, although I look white?"

I backtracked. She did look white. In an emotionless monotone, she talked about the ugliness of racism while I thought of appearances and illusions. "What Was, Was Not" could have been the movie title of the past week. Everyone thought beautiful Johanna was happy, loyal, and rich. Everyone thought that Diego was devotedly in love with his wife, the model husband who worked to make his wife's career possible. The Lincoln Center fountain was just a water gargler, then became a deadly weapon, then turned out to be just a fountain after all. Greenhouse made beautiful love while he weighed the possibilities of an ex-wife. The list of illusions was probably endless. I left the TV woman to keep herself company and started walking briskly. I wanted to be home, snuggled up in bed, asleep.

At the corner I stopped, thinking I heard footsteps behind me. A man walked by, his body curved, his head low. He was cold too. I walked behind him, trying to keep his fast pace, glad of his presence. We came to a block-long building whose ground floor was boarded up with plywood layered with torn posters and ads. I looked up at the third floor. The lamp from the cross street curved into the paneless corner windows, giving the half-gutted black building one bright eye. The footsteps I was following stopped. I looked down.

My man had gone. He's turned the corner, I thought, resigning myself to go the rest of the way alone. I wasn't scared really, just lonely.

Near the end of the block, the plywood covering was gone, leaving a gaping black opening. I thought of the Times Square man with his shiny new boots and his cardboard home. With enough plywood he could build himself a shack. But where would he put it? Not inside this awful, plunging hole.

An arm grabbed my waist and pushed me inside. I screamed and stumbled over something hard—a brick, some plaster. A hand clamped my mouth and my chin, cutting my scream with the sharpness of scissors. I kicked as hard as I could, my arms flailing behind me, trying to grab whoever was holding me. He shifted his grasp over my arms, my chest, squeezing my ribs, his hand so large over my face I could barely breathe. I struggled and heaved in complete panic. My fingers tried to pinch his thighs. My feet kicked his ankles, his shins. It was a feeble defense but the only one I had. Oh God, I thought, Johanna! I'm going to end up like Johanna!

"Shh, shh," the man whispered in my ear, now rocking his body sideways as if to calm me. He lowered his hand, letting me inhale. *"Non ti faccio male."*

Massimo. Massimo saying he wasn't going to harm me. He grasped me tighter and turned us around, pushing deeper into the gutted building. His feet stumbled while he heaved me up, trying to avoid my kicking legs. As we turned a corner that blotted out all light, I went limp, hoping he'd relax his hold. I was dizzy, petrified.

"Listen, god damn it! I'll make you listen!" He

gave my mouth a slap, jerking my head back against his shoulder. His hand smelled of expensive cologne. He was going to kill me with perfumed hands.

"I loved her. I loved her more than any of the other women. But it didn't work. It just didn't work. Do you understand? Do you know what that's like? Of course not, you're a woman. All you have to do is open your legs and groan. Lie! That's all you have to do!" His lips touched my ear. "Lie!" I could feel his spit spraying me. "I can never know if you liked it, can I?" He turned me around and pushed me against a wall, his hand still on my mouth. His knees pinned me down. It was too dark to see him. All I sensed was the smell of his cologne and his body, desperately firm. And my own sweating fear.

"Do you understand?" He waited, his chest heaving. I shook my head slowly.

"It didn't work for me. No matter what I or she did, my penis was useless. She asked me to bind her, slap her around. I thought she was doing it for me, to give me an erection. It took me weeks to realize she got pleasure out of it. She said she liked it that I couldn't penetrate her. It made her feel clean." He'd moved away from me now, holding only my mouth, pushing my head back against the stripped-down roughness of the wall. With a jerk I might be free. As if sensing my thoughts he stroked my cheekbone with his free hand. A surprising gesture.

"Please listen to me. Please!" He relaxed his hand on my mouth. My chapped lips stuck to his palm.

"I wanted to slap you around, scare you. Do to you what I wanted to do to Johanna. Here in the dark. In this filth where she belonged." He lowered his hand and I heard him step back. "Don't go, Simona. Listen to me. I won't hurt you. I have to tell someone. I trust you, Simona. You'll keep quiet and you'll help. You'll find out for me."

I didn't move.

"At the beginning of the film, Johanna promised to marry me. She was happy, declaring that we were going to be a romantic, virginal couple. Then her mood would change, and she'd call me 'a worn-out, useless prick.' But she always said we would get married. The day we got to New York she took me to her bedroom and, lying there naked, told me what her father had done to her." Massimo exhaled a trembling breath. "She said she enjoyed it, that it made her feel loved. Being filled with the same semen that created her was the most natural love in the world. That's the kind of shit her father told her. She was her mother's reincarnation, he told her, too beautiful to be touched by anyone else. Johanna cried all night after that confession. She wanted me to make it go away. What could I do?"

"Get her some professional help." And what does one do to her father's kind? Kill them? Strip them slowly of their sexual parts? Find enough love for the human race to understand? I felt only a thick, hardening anger. I still didn't move.

"She told me she could only marry an impotent man. It would make her father happy. That's what she deserved, she said. An impotent man." Massimo was gasping now, crying, I thought.

"I wanted to show her what good love was like, but I couldn't. I haven't been able to make love to anyone for years. The world thinks I'm this great

Latin Lover . . ." he sniffed loudly ". . . that I love them and leave them. I'm the one who gets left. First they wait, then they mother, then they have affairs with others, then they give up and leave."

"You're lucky," I said. "Those frustrated lovers kept their mouths shut."

"Women can be good that way." Massimo moved away. I could hear his steps crunching plaster, clanking empty cans. "Not Johanna. She was going to tell *People.*" His voice came from far away. I felt cold.

"That's what she told me at your party." He raised his voice. "She was going to tell the whole world I couldn't get it up!" He picked up something and hurled it at the wall behind me. I turned toward the pinging sound and, in a corner, saw an empty foil container scoop up a ray of street lamp. Beyond it, black faded into gray. The street was in that direction, to my left, behind me. I took a step as quietly as I could. Then another. A car stopped nearby, and I moved quickly.

"No, no, you have to listen, you have to help me." Massimo stopped me, holding my arm. I screamed.

A long beam of light cut across the space and found my eyes, then shifted to my right.

"Police. Don't move. I've got you covered with a gun." It was Greenhouse. I could barely make out a crouched figure to the left of the flashlight. Raf held the beam steady on Massimo, who peered into that white halo with a dirty, tear-stained face. In the bowels of that gutted building, he had turned into an old, broken man. I waved an arm in front of me.

"It's OK. I'm all right," I found myself saying,

suddenly convinced Massimo was in too much pain to hurt anyone. "We were just having a talk."

"Why the hell did you scream?" Greenhouse stayed crouched, gun pointed. I held my hand in front of Massimo's face to interrupt the flashlight's beam. What he was going through was no business of the police.

"I stumbled. Come on, Greenhouse, let up."

Raf panned the beam toward the exit. I grabbed Massimo's hand and walked out. Raf and Greenhouse followed. I blinked under the street lamp, welcoming the sight of the newly laid asphalt shimmering with specks of recycled glass.

"What were you doing in there?" Greenhouse asked, pointing his gun toward the dark hole we'd just left.

"Why were you following me? Look, I appreciate your concern, but I can take care of myself."

"No, you can't!" he yelled. "You get all fizzed up with some stupid idea, and off you go like a crazed champagne cork bumping into everything until you find what you want. You could have gotten raped in that rat hole, gotten AIDS, gotten killed!" He banged his gun-holding fist against the car roof. "Stay home and let the police do their job!"

Greenhouse looked at the gun in his hand and dropped it back in his shoulder holster, avoiding my face. Raf walked in front of the car and got into the driver's seat. Massimo breathed heavily somewhere to my right.

"Come on, I'll take you home," Greenhouse said with a sideways nod. His voice was bossy but back in control.

"No, I'll take myself home. I don't need you to save me or take me home."

Greenhouse flung the back door open, his face bull-pawing mad. "You want into my life? That's what you said, right? Well, this is it." He waved me inside.

Instantly I wanted to hug him, to stick my nose into the warmth of his neck, to kiss him, to make love to him right there, in that back seat. Behind me Massimo moved, and Diego, Sara, Johanna buzzed around my head again. I remembered what it was like to be left without strength.

"I need to walk," I said, hoping he'd understand.

Greenhouse slammed the door and got in the passenger side, brandishing a tough New York City cop face. Raf leaned over and handed me a note. By the look he gave me, he wasn't loving me either.

Raf turned the motor on and shifted into gear; Greenhouse rolled down the window. "Your friend Toni may be all right. A witness has been called who's willing to testify that he saw Sam Weston electrify the Lincoln Center fountain."

"But Jonathan said . . ." My words got buried under the furious squeal of wheels taking off into the vast black horizon. Very responsible, grown-up behavior.

Massimo sat down on the curb and buried his head in his hands. I snapped.

"Damn it, Massimo! Don't you ever grab a woman like that in your life. That 'rat hole' could have been full of crack addicts glinting knives for a quarter. Next time you have to get something off your chest, select a comfortable, well-lighted living room, will you? God, you've been acting so long you can't talk without the right stage set!"

Massimo looked back at the skeletal building.

"I've lost all hope." His head hit his knees.

"And stop moaning your fate! Do something about it! There has to be a reason. Find out what it is. Try doctors, psychiatrists. If the first one doesn't have the answer, keep trying! Don't just give up and play victim for the rest of your life. Do you hear?" I was crouching, shaking his sleeve. "Come on, Massimo, you said it. 'Go, go, go, the American way. Everything an active verb.' "

Massimo turned and gave me his signature smile, this time with an added droop of eyelids.

I joined him on the curb. "Why did you think I could help?"

"That reporter. I have to know if Johanna told him about me. I'm getting old, my hair's falling out, I'm hanging on to my career by my capped teeth. She can't ruin me. She just can't!"

"She didn't say anything. She didn't get a chance to."

"I didn't kill her."

"No, I don't think you did," I said, going by a gut feeling that would have made Greenhouse groan. I fished in my pocket for Raf's note. I glanced quickly through the list of things found near Johanna's body, knowing I didn't need it anymore. At the bottom of the note, written in a thin spidery handwriting I could barely make out, Raf gave me the latest news about Abe.

The D.A.'s office had gone looking for Abe after Raf had told them about Sam's marriage certificate. He'd been found in a cabin in Jackson Hole with a new girlfriend. No television, no newspapers. Just nature, frozen food mixed with freshly caught trout, and sex. Abe admitted that when he'd seen Sam cut a gash in the electric cable and put the cable on the drain valve, he saw his chance for a paid vacation. He kicked the cable away from the valve, stuck his hand in the water and pretended to fry.

Sam, the killer after all? I looked at the list again, at the letter, at the asphalt sparkling under the street lamps. Oh, damn, damn, damn.

"Get up," I commanded, getting on my feet. Massimo looked at me, surprised by my tone. "We're going home." Massimo obeyed.

"I tried a doctor," he said. "Nothing. Nothing is physically wrong."

"Try another." I didn't care anymore.

"I tried a psychiatrist too." We walked towards Sixth Avenue under the wider lights of Houston. A steady flow of headlights crossed each other going east and west. "He explained that I really wanted to be a girl because my father preferred my sister."

I stopped in front of Arturo's. The smell of pizza mixed with the low jazz sounds of a trumpet. I wanted to stay glued to that spot.

"I paid the preposterous bill and left." Massimo walked on and I followed slowly, hoping to postpone what faced me.

"The sister theory isn't one you accept?" I asked.

"I have no sister." He tried out a laugh that didn't work very well. "Besides, I enjoy the privileges of manhood even in this condition."

"In America, a public confession is the thing," I said. "You tell your public your problem. They will listen, sympathize, support you." We reached Sixth Avenue.

"What is private should stay private." Massimo said, extending an arm to hail a cab. On the corner, behind a high cyclone fence, a small group of boys and men played basketball. A few passersby watched, others sat on benches drinking out of paper bags. A couple of men lay on the sidewalk, either asleep or passed out. A cab stopped in the middle of the avenue. The car behind it honked and swerved.

Massimo hesitated. "Forgive me?"

"I'm alive," I said. I wouldn't let him kiss my cheeks. I crumbled Raf's note in my pocket and bit my lip. God, I didn't want to see the truth.

The driver leaned toward the window and yelled, "You want a cab or don't ya?"

Massimo ran to the door and opened it. I ran too and slipped inside.

"I'll ride with you to the Royalton," I told his surprised face.

He got in after me and closed the door. We lurched against the back of the seat as the driver took off

"Your company helps. Thanks," Massimo said. He'd completely misunderstood.

Chapter Thirteen

Sara opened her hotel door only halfway. She squinted at me, her face bare of sunglasses. "What's the matter, Simona? You look like the Phantom *sans* mask." Barefoot, knobby-kneed, barely dressed in a short, corn-yellow cotton bathrobe, she clung to the door.

"I need to talk." I pushed the door open and walked into a small room cramped with avantgarde furniture and mundane layers of male and female clothing. Four gaping leather suitcases overlapped on the metal-horned king-size bed. A slim burnished wood closet hung open to show Diego's elegant jackets. I stepped over shoes, moved a contorted bundle of black tights from a giraffe-like metal chair, and sat down. A few inches from my nose, on a pale wood inverted pyramid, Sara's boots leaned against the spidery chrome legs of a lamp. Two airline tickets stuck out from under a heel.

"Where's Diego?"

"He's gone to Times Square to get the Italian papers."

"Good. I know about the B and B, Sara."

"What do you know?" Sara began lifting

clothes, circling the restricted space, looking for something.

"Come on, don't make me say it."

Sara whipped around, glossy lingerie slipping from her fingers. "Why do you care?" She sat down on the coffee table, a sharp triangle of glass and metal. "Haven't you heard? The lawyer said *tutto* OK for Toni. Sam, football Sam, first tried to kill Johanna at Lincoln Center. He scored the second time. They were married once or something." She sliced the air with a flat hand, a gesture she used on the set to mean "it's a wrap."

"It's not over, Sara, because I don't believe he killed her. I think he put a gash in that cable to scare her. He got her in his arms, he carried her to the trailer, maybe he thought she'd be eternally grateful. Sam wouldn't try to kill her in front of all those spectators. Too many things could go wrong. He'd choose a simpler way."

"Copper wire. Very simple." Sara had got up again, resumed her hunt.

"Tell me about it."

"What are you saying?" Her hands pecked and discarded. Her face stayed down.

"I'm here to listen. That's all I can do. Tell me about finding out."

Sara shook her head, an expression of extreme sadness on her face. "Why, Simona? I'm barely holding myself together. Leave it alone."

I couldn't allow myself to care. "That's not what you taught me in the dubbing studio. 'Don't let anything go,' you'd say, when the actor was tired or not good enough and I was about to settle for second best. 'Seek the best, always the best,' you urged, even if it meant reducing someone to anger or tears. Now I'm doing just that, seeking the best take, the one that makes the most sense. The truth."

Sara reached over my head and shook out a lizard boot. A pair of glasses fell on my lap. The V ones for Victory and Varni. She slipped them on and sat back on the glass triangle, overlapping her kimono over thick, muscled thighs.

"When did you find out?" I asked.

"I noticed the place in the phone book. I liked the 'Bed and Breakfast with a SoHo Artist' line." She fingered the full ashtray on the carpet, picked out a longish butt and lit it. "The implications were interesting for such a Puritan country." Gray ash colored her lips. She wasn't going to give, and for a second I asked myself what I was doing. Why didn't I just go to the police? No, that would be a betrayal. She had to be the one to go. I had come to give her that push.

"Pretend it's a movie, Sara. There's this woman director, not young any more, devoted to her husband, believing he's equally devoted to her. Through the years they have become famous as a team. Many say that without her, the husband would be just another restless rich boy dabbling without results. A few, those who know her closely, say she would never have achieved fame without him. They say he captures her genius and releases it at the right time, in the right dosage. This couple, so vitally tied together, make a film, and she discovers he's about to leave her for the lead actress. Maybe she finds out because she overhears a phone call. Maybe she finds a strange New York number scribbled on a pad and investigates. We could write a hundred different ways of how she finds out. The important thing is that she knows. There is the added painful irony that her

208

producer-husband has convinced her to use this well-known Hollywood actress because of her box-office draw. The actress is paid five million dollars, a sum unheard of for a director who prides herself for making small budget films and thumbing her nose at Hollywood. The director accepted only because she trusted her husband, because he said that with one harmless compromise they would make tons of money. After that, they could make all the ideological films she wanted, together. I think the director feels betrayed on many fronts. To bring matters to a head, the lead actress tells Barbara Walters she's giving an exclusive to *People*. What if she decides to talk about the producer's love for her? Then everyone would know. And if everyone knows, there's no more denying, no more salvaging the heart, the bed, the reputation." I stood up. "If you were writing the screenplay, Sara, a truthful screenplay, how would you have it end? Would the director suffer in silence for the rest of her life, or would she try to control the ending by killing off the star? What would be more in character?"

Sara stuck her hands between her bare thighs and looked at me, some of her old spunk back in her face. "That's Hollywood crap!"

"Why did you have to kill her? You could have kicked her off the film, told Diego to go to hell, taken a lover, I don't know what else." I swept the boots off the bureau. Sara stood up. "Damn it! Why did you have to kill her?"

Sara gripped my shoulder. "Stay out if it, Simona! Walk out of this hotel room, go to your American lover and forget this. Forget us. Toni is OK, you are OK. What do you care?" She gripped harder, hurting me. "What the *cazzo* do you care about that tramp and who killed her? I would have gutted her, that's what I would have done!" She was spitting in my face, shaking me. "Ripped her open and hanged her by a hook, like the cow she was!"

I jerked her hand off my shoulder. "Instead you used a nice medieval method, a copper tourniquet twisted around the neck with the help of a long nail: Where'd you get the nail? From Sam's toolbox along with the wire? Or from that construction site in Spanish Harlem where you probably stole the hard hat and the jacket you used to get into the Majestic? Come on, Sara, you've always been big on Truth with a capital T in your films. Let's have some now."

She sat back on the small triangle of glass, hunched over. I picked up her boots from the bureau and searched inside each one. I got on my knees and started looking inside Diego's shoes. I was looking for another pair of Sara's glasses. The rhinestone ones. Sara followed me with her eyes. Her face had turned into a festering wound.

I found them wrapped in a chenille scarf in a pocket of her overnight case. They were still held together by a safety pin. "These glasses gave you away, Sara. When I found Johanna's body, something was glinting in the carpet next to her. I thought it was one of her diamond earrings. I was wrong." I scrambled in my pocket for Raf's list. "Read for yourself. The item under 'one six-inch nail.'" Sara grabbed the sheet, lifting her sunglasses to read.

"'One large rhinestone the size of a raisin,'" I quoted, holding up the broken glasses to the ceiling light. "I'll bet anything that rhinestone will fit right in here." Sara lunged for my arm. I jumped

210

back against the wall and pocketed the glasses. She leaned forward in a desperate reach, lost her balance, and fell against the chair. Her glasses fell off her forehead, she fumbled for them and lost her grip on the chair. She slid to a crunching halt on the floor, on top of her Varni-Victory sunglasses. *"Cazzo!"* she screamed.

"What is it, Sara?" Diego asked as the door opened in my face.

Sara quickly ran her hands through her short hair and straightened herself up. "I broke another pair of glasses. And Simona . . ." she hesitated and looked at me, a last plea on her face. Diego closed the door and peered at me in surprise. ". . . . Simona needs money."

He dropped a bundle of papers on the chair and reached into his breast pocket. "Of course, I promised her a bonus." He extracted a pair of plain Ray-Bans and handed them to Sara in an automatic gesture that told me he'd done it a hundred times. My stomach somersaulted, splashing the taste of acid up my throat. "You always carry a spare," I mumbled, my mouth so burning dry I could hardly get the words out.

Diego took a checkbook from the inside pocket of his jacket. "A spare?"

"Glasses. You always carry a spare set of glasses for Sara." Saliva started coming back to my mouth as thoughts pumped into my brain. "The day Johanna was murdered, Sara was wearing her American flag glasses, not the rhinestone ones. And you wore the same cashmere blazer you'd worn the night before at my party when you'd slipped Sara's broken rhinestone glasses in your pocket. The glasses must have still been in your pocket. That's how the rhinestone got into the

211

bedroom. Johanna struggled before she died. She overturned a chair. She might have knocked the glasses out of your pocket, or they fell out as you bent over her. Sara didn't kill Johanna. You did!"

An openhanded slap sent me reeling against the closet door. The door swung closed, and I fell into the closet. Diego was on top of me, his full weight against my chest. I hiked up my knee as hard as I could at his crotch and centered. He gasped, lifted his hips in pain, and shifted slightly, enough for me to slip from under him. I had nowhere to go. His body blocked the narrow corridor between the closet and the bed. I put my head under the bed and started crawling on my stomach. He grabbed both my hips and pulled me back until my legs were halfway up the inside of the closet. He turned me around, his hands circling my throat, his square jaw gnashing. I twisted my head trying to free myself, feeling my skin tearing under his fingers, his weight blocking my breath. My knees struggled against heavy thighs pinning me down. My hips heaved against the furious weight of his torso. My eyes were scorching. Black shapes began to waver in front of my face. A stream rushed in my ears. I grabbed air with a free fist.

A long screech shattered my ear. This is it. This is the brain exploding, the neck breaking in two. Death.

It was Sara. Blessed, wonderful Sara with her terrible voice and her new pistol aimed at Diego's head. For a few dizzy moments, I let air seep into my lungs and tried not to swallow. Diego lifted himself up to lean against the closet. My body was finally free, except for his calves resting on my thighs for lack of space.

"One death is enough," Sara said in a calmer

voice. "How do I call the police, Simona?"

I crawled under the bed and came out the other side. My mouth dripped grateful drops of blood all over my heaving bosom and the four-hundred-dollar-a-night carpet. I lifted myself slowly; rigor mortis hadn't decided whether to come or go. My neck had been replaced by a cozy circle of fire. All that was missing were the marshmallows. I managed to dial 911 for the second time that week. While we waited for the police, Diego kept his head in the shadow of the closet door and refused to speak. All I could see of his upper body was part of a camel hair jacket, a blue silk shirt, and a stunning Ferragamo tie. As my mother would have said, always dress nicely, you never know what may happen.

Sara talked. She claimed she always "felt my husband in my every vein." After Johanna's death, she had confronted Diego, suspecting he might have killed her. Diego confessed, confident she would never betray him. He had met Johanna a year ago in Sardinia on a Milanese industrialist's yacht. After that first sunbaked meeting, Johanna had pursued him with phone calls, notes, sudden visits to Rome. She wanted him at all costs. She loved him madly.

"Diego saw a golden opportunity and offered her the film." Half-hidden by her V glasses, Sara looked strong. She told Diego's story as if it were just another of her fictions, the only difference being that this story was spoken, not seen.

"The only way Johanna would agree to play the role was if Diego said he loved her, if he would spend some nights with her. No lovemaking. She didn't want that. He agreed but didn't tell me, of course. She wouldn't have got anywhere near my

213

camera if I'd known."

"What about the five million dollars?"

"She insisted on that absurd amount because that's what those two were supposed to live on. They were both going to give up the movies and live on a farm. She wanted to raise sheep in New Zealand. Diego, a sheep farmer!" Sara came as close to a laugh as she could manage under the circumstances.

"Meanwhile, my sentimental husband swears he was only thinking of our film. He got his snotty family to lend him some money, thanks to Johanna's box office fame, and gave her five million dollars without blinking, convinced he was going to make mountains of money in the end. Whenever Diego came to New York for 'money-raising meetings,' they'd meet at that SoHo place. He was afraid an indiscreet camera might catch him coming and going to the Majestic at odd hours." Sara stood up, handed me the gun, and pulled on a pair of black tights from the pile on the floor. I slipped my finger gently over the trigger, not letting on that I had no idea how to use the thing.

"They made love in SoHo. *Finally!* Titillated by raindrops on the windowpane and paint-stained walls or some such crap." She dropped the kimono, showing wide muscular shoulders and small, slack breasts. She reached for a black sweater under a suitcase. "Penetration by Diego and the woman went gaga, wanted to marry him, said she wouldn't finish the film if he didn't leave me immediately." The enormous sweater slipped over her tanned arms, her ruffled head, and settled on her shoulders, making her instantly look smaller. "I don't know what came over her. He's not *that* good." Obviously one thing Diego had kept back was Johanna's history of abuse.

"Anyway, she threatened to tell *People*. When he got furious, she backed off and wrote him a check for the famous five million. She wanted to prove how much she loved him." Sara popped her head in front of the bathroom mirror, combing her hair with her fingers. "I pity her. I hated her alive. Now I can afford to pity her. Horrible, but there it is. This whole story is so trite I can't even make a meaningful movie out of it." She slipped on the tiger glasses she'd found in her vanity case, took the gun from my hands and went back to her perch on the triangle table. Still barefoot, she looked ready for anything. I ached too much to move.

Diego shifted until the ceiling spot hit his face. Staring at Sara with his deep, almost hidden eyes, he looked powerful even in defeat.

"I did not love her, and I did not wish you to leave me."

Sara raised the gun with both hands to shoulder level, as if about to shoot. Diego stared back, not budging. "You liked the idea of having it all," she said. "Being of a simple, one-track mind, you killed her and pocketed the check, probably counting on cashing it in Switzerland after someone else had been conveniently found guilty of Johanna's murder. You probably even thought her death would bring more money to the box office. Your family was right all along. You are worthless."

"If you left me," he craned his neck forward, the rest of him immobile, "then, yes, I would be worthless. That is the reason I killed her."

"You're crazy," I blurted out, feeling safe with Sara's gun pointed at him. A knock at the door stopped me from elaborating. A discreet voice with an English accent said, "Ma'am, the police you requested are here," as if they were part of room service.

"Un momento," Sara yelled. With one hand she reached for her lizard boots and wriggled them on. "Get up," she told Diego. "Look like a man." He followed instructions, smoothing his hair, his camel jacket. He even tried smiling at her. I looked away, repulsed.

Sari handed me the gun. "Tuck it away somewhere. The safety's back on."

"I'm forever grateful, Sara, but why'd you wait so long to use this thing?" I asked, slipping the heavy, warm metal into my pocket. "My brains were about to get squirted on the wall."

"I couldn't find it in this mess." One last look in the bathroom mirror and she opened the door for the police.

Epilogue

The assistant D.A. dropped the charges against Toni and shifted his rookie zeal to Diego. The Park Avenue lawyer who originally was going to defend Toni accepted Diego's case and has advised him to plead temporary insanity. Diego's family has publicly stated that Diego's downfall was a direct result of "consorting with Leftist politicians and the debauched movie world." They will not pay a cent toward his defense. Sara flew back to Rome to ask for help, and the movie world friends who supposedly led Diego to kill came forth with a generous check. The lawyer accepted the check, but also insisted on a share of the profits of *Where Goes the Future?*

Sara's back in New York now to stick close to Diego, who had to surrender his passport. "As you said, he's crazy," she told me when I met her at the airport, "but he killed someone to keep me. I can't leave him now."

"I suppose it has something to do with obsessions," I ventured, trying to understand the Sara Varni logic.

She rewarded me with a subdued *"brava,"* and a pat on the cheek.

Her film editor has flown back with her and the three of them are locked up at HearView, as if nothing had happened, trying to get the film cut to Sara's satisfaction. They're now aiming for a more realistic Easter release. Diego's trial is scheduled for January.

Last week I did get a chance to lure Sara away from the moviola long enough to treat her to that garlic pizza Raf raved about at Orso's. After the great pizza and before the *penne all'arrabbiata* (which means: done the angry way), I asked her when she'd found out about Johanna and Diego.

"Men can be divided into two camps: those who cheat and get nasty, and those who cheat and get sweet. Diego was far too attentive this past year. Presents, caresses, he tried to explain his every movement. I suspected but decided to ignore it. I was too busy with the film to face that possibility.

"When we got to New York that first day I went into his wallet to tip room service and found that Bed & Breakfast card. Johanna, I thought. Don't ask me why. Some conversation I don't remember, something I saw that I didn't connect until that 'Bed and Breakfast with the SoHo artists' stared in my face. I don't know how these intuitions work, but they do work. I pictured beautiful, sensual Johanna and my uterus shriveled up and died. So much so I didn't say anything. A big mistake. Had I confronted him, he wouldn't have killed her. But then maybe I too wanted her dead. Who knows?"

She spoke of *Where Goes the Future?* for the rest of the meal. Her eyes were hidden behind a new pair of sunglasses: two squares with a row of small, rectangular holes on each vertical side next to which small numbers had been printed. The glasses looked like two frames of negative film. I paid the check and she stood up. "It is hard to accept that I can scream *'cazzo'* till Venice dries up, and still not control the outcome of Diego's trial." Inside the lobby of the HearView building, she added, "There must be a way to bring a coherent, political message into this mess so I can make a film of it." As I watched the elevator door close on her waving good-bye, I had no doubt Sara'd make a prizewinning film out of the whole sordid story.

Massimo is in Hollywood doing another picture offered to him after his name hit the headlines with Johanna's death. This time he's a Colombian drug lord who repents and turns his colleagues in. Hollywood obviously thinks Italian and Spanish accents sound the same. He asked me to be his dialogue coach when the offer came through, but I said no. The two weeks' vacation was up, and I had to go back to my advertising job. Besides, I've had enough of movies for a while. He did go to another doctor in Hollywood. For a bad case of laryngitis. The specialist told Massimo he was too nervous and suggested he take tranquilizers. Massimo confessed he'd been taking Inderal for years to help him with stage fright. Afraid the jitters might come at any time, he began swallowing the pills down like saliva even when he wasn't acting. Of course he hadn't mentioned this to any doctor. What would it look like if anyone knew the great Massimo Marini popped downers to keep him suave? No doctor was needed; he'd heard about the drug from an actress, and his supply came from his housekeeper's admiring daughter, who worked in a pharmacy. What the actress had not told him, and Massimo had not bothered to read in the small print, was that in very rare cases Inderal can cause impotency.

The other day UPS delivered a huge bottle of Giorgio, bought on Rodeo Drive. There was no message, just a barely legible "Massimo" taking up half the card. Something tells me he'd had a successful date the night before.

I haven't seen Sam since that day at the airport. I called him to apologize about being so unrelenting with him. He heard me out, mumbled "No sweat," and hung up. Raf let me know that Sam challenged Abe's story, and Abe finally admitted that although he had seen Sam nick the cable and place the exposed part on the drain valve, Abe hadn't been the one to kick the cable away. Sam had done it himself, changing his mind just before the first take. Why Sam wanted to electrify the fountain in the first place, I don't know. Neither do the police. Did he actually want to kill her? I don't believe it. For all his gruff manners, I think Sam is very gentle. I'm sure he just wanted to play hero one more night for Johanna.

Toni is in Oxford, Mississipi, snapping photos with his Leica. At least that's where he was the last time he sent me a postcard. He doesn't call, never lets me know where he's staying. I have no way of reaching him. "He's on the road," Jonathan says, "Kerouac style." I wonder how long Toni will have to run before Johanna begins to fade.

Jonathan did an article on Johanna for *People*. It was, as he had promised, a gentleman's rendition of her life, written with boyish awe. He mentioned that I found her dead, but didn't ask for or invent any gossipy details. He's come over a couple of times. We eat, we talk about the photo book, about Toni, about New York. We've become friends. Sometimes he wonders what confession Johanna was going to make to *People*. I think of her father's sexual abuse, and keep my mouth shut. Her story might have helped countless other women and girls, but she isn't here to tell it, and no one else has a right to it.

Christmas is two weeks away, and I'd love to see the Rockefeller Center tree under a thick coating of snow. I bought a necklace of cultured pearls for Tiffany to add to her collection. A blow-up of Johanna is already hanging on Tiffany's closet door. Saturday I'm taking her for a round of Christmas-window gazing, starting at Tiffany's.

I've seen Greenhouse once since that night on Mercer Street. We did a lot of talking over chili and frozen margaritas. He told me he'd never wanted to go back to Irene. Willy had almost flunked out of school the year before, and a psychologist had blamed it on a delayed reaction to the divorce. A combination of guilt and love had made him think remarriage to Irene was a possibility.

"For all of five minutes," he said, laughing. He's admitted finally that he's scared of falling in love, and he's not sure he has enough space in his life for someone as "eruptive" as I. Being compared to a volcano is something I like. That's how I feel these days: strong and massive. That could be because I've gained a few pounds that don't worry me for once. As for being "eruptive," *cazzo*, that's the fun of life!

Greenhouse would like to go on seeing me, but I'm not ready. I'm afraid I'd fall back on my leaning-tower-of-Pisa habits. I'm enjoying my no-involvement time. I'm beginning to explore the things I like to do, what I want to be, without worrying about pleasing "him." I miss Greenhouse, I am probably in love with him, but for once I want to come first. I go out a lot with friends from the office. I've seen plays, movies, read a slew of books. Inspired by Toni and Jonathan, I'm even thinking of writing a cookbook.

My upstairs neighbor Tania is back from Japan. She's been living alone for ten years and loving it. She thinks I'm learning fast for an Italian. Her family, parents and three younger sisters are coming to New York for Christmas, and I'm cooking up a four-course meal in the Italian tradition. For New Year's we're all going back to their home in Vermont.

I'm beginning to understand that where the future goes is up to me. I'm scared and lonely at times, but that won't stop me from taking hold of my life. After all, to do the impossible is the American way.

Insalata u' Pisci Bbonu

(Sicilian Good Fish Salad)

For 4 servings

19-oz. can of cannellini beans
15-oz. can of corn kernels
heart of celery sliced very thin — about 2 cups
bunch scallions sliced — green part included
½ red pepper diced very small (for color)
hearts of palm sliced (optional)
1-inch tuna steak or 2 cans of light meat tuna
large basil leaves

Dressing:

½ tbsp. balsamic vinegar or 1 tbsp. lemon juice
according to preference
tbsp. extra virgin olive oil
salt and pepper
clove of minced garlic.

Drain the beans and the corn, and put in a
serving bowl. Add sliced celery, scallions, red pepper, hearts of palm. If using tuna steak, sear it in
very hot skillet three minutes per side. Let cool
and slice. Add to bowl. If using canned tuna,

drain and add. Tear basil leaves into small piece
and add to bowl.

In a small bowl mix salt, pepper and garlic to
lemon juice or balsamic vinegar. Add olive oil
Whip together well, pour in tuna bowl, and gently
mix all ingredients. Serve at room temperature
with hearty bread and chilled white wine. *Buor
appetito!*